Eternity
Falls

Also by Frank Sherry

Raiders and Rebels

Pacific Passions

The Devil's Captain

Eternity Falls

Frank Sherry

iUniverse, Inc.
Bloomington

Eternity Falls

iUniverse books may be ordered through booksellers or by contacting:

iUniverse
1663 Liberty Drive
Bloomington, IN 47403
www.iuniverse.com
1-800-Authors (1-800-288-4677)

ISBN: 978-1-4759-6204-8 (sc)
ISBN: 978-1-4759-6202-4 (e)
ISBN: 978-1-4759-6203-1 (dj)

Library of Congress Control Number: 2012921692

Printed in the United States of America

iUniverse rev. date: 1/7/2013

This book is for Su, Stephen, Diana, and Meg,
whom I love, and whom I know love me.

CHAPTER 1

G ABRIEL FIRST DETECTED WORDS in the waterfall on the day he learned of his brother's illness. But the chain of events that led him to that discovery had begun earlier that day—with a nightmare that invaded his afternoon sleep.

The dream had commenced with an image of innocence: Two boys, one about seven years old, the other about five, are standing on the side of a dirt road somewhere in the country. The boys are dressed alike in navy-blue shorts, sandals, and starched white shirts. The older boy is skinny. A shock of gold-red hair falls over his blue eyes. The other boy is dark-haired and chunky. Gabriel recognizes the younger boy as his brother, Michael, the elder as his own boy-self, young Gabe. Slowly, in the way of dreams, he becomes young Gabe again—and with this transition the vision turns sinister.

Two larger-than-life figures, a male and a female, appear on the road. Sensing malignity in them, young Gabe clasps his brother's hand in his. The hulking figures, robed in black from head to foot, have no faces. They float toward young Gabe and his brother, but young Gabe knows it is him they want. Why do these giants have no faces? He wants to run, but he can't move. Around him the pines whisper to each other. He feels the heat of the sun, the presence of evil. The giants halt before him and Michael. He sees that their robes are not garments after all but emptiness where the light can't penetrate. It comes to him that the creatures within that blackness have no faces because they don't wish him to recognize them.

1

The male figure's arm, pale as a fish belly, stretches forth out of the blackness. Elongated fingers point. The female also points. Young Gabe knows he has done evil: stolen, lied, and disobeyed. He can't remember exactly what he's done, but he cries out, "I'm sorry! I won't do it again!" The giants turn and shrink themselves into a car. The car starts. Trailing dust, it carries them down the road. Young Gabe hates them. He wishes them dead.

The car suddenly explodes. The wreckage burns in the middle of the road. The giants slouch within it as the blaze consumes them. Young Gabe rejoices to see them incinerated. But then remorse crushes his heart—for he loves them and he knows that his wish has caused them to burn. He begins to cry. His brother says, "It's okay, Gabe. They were bad to us."

Here the nightmare had collapsed. Gabriel had opened his eyes to a familiar bedroom suffused with light. He was again Gabriel Fallon, a man of fifty-four, a writer who no longer wrote, a man contemplating an end to his wasted life. Damp with sweat, he lay fully clothed on the bed. The sun flooded through the room's windows, left curtainless because Thea, his wife, possessed no drapes large enough to cover their expanse. The clock on the dresser said 2:17. Gabriel had been asleep for less than an hour. He felt his arrhythmic heart (a case of atrial fibrillation) flopping within his rib cage. To calm it, he sat up on the side of the bed and took a series of deep breaths.

Gabriel stared out the windows at the woods, where shafts of light filtered through the hemlocks and maples, all rich with greenery on this Thursday in June. Summer had finally arrived in the Catskills, where Gabriel and Thea had been living for the past ten months—in a house that resembled a ski lodge more than a dwelling.

He took his pulse and found it still erratic. Why had this nightmare set his heart galloping so? Was it because he recognized the giants as manifestations of his despair—as demons bent on torturing him even in sleep with images of his botched existence? Or was it the presence of Michael in the dream that had unsettled him? But why would that be so?

Gabriel and his brother had gone their separate ways long ago—each of them seeing in the other a reminder of their toxic childhood. Michael, a grandfather now, lived with his second wife in the Missouri Ozarks. For twenty-five years he and Gabriel had had little contact with each other. Except for the funerals of their parents, they had met face-to-face only once in that quarter century at a dinner party six years ago. Since then Gabriel had not even talked to Michael on the phone. And yet young Michael had made his way into Gabriel's nightmare. Was Michael, like the giants, also a demon of despair?

His heart slowing at last, Gabriel rose from the bed and went into the hallway. He paused. Except for the sound of the waterfall outside, the house was silent. Was Thea taking a nap? She sometimes stretched out on the couch in the study just down the hall. Gabriel peeped into the room. Empty. But the answering machine on the desk was flashing. He entered and pushed the message button. The tape clicked on: "Gabriel, this is Beth. Call me. As soon as you can. I have to talk to you." The voice clicked off. The red eye of the machine stared as if warning of calamity ahead.

The Beth on the tape was Gabriel's sister, Elizabeth. At forty, she was fourteen years younger than Gabriel. She lived in Seattle, where she was a photographer with a reputation for catching in her lens what the galleries called the gritty images of urban life: the homeless, the leather boys, the whores, and the befuddled. Beth had also acquired credentials as a licensed psychologist, though she practiced only intermittently. "I'm too much interested in myself to do much good for others," she said. She had never married and swore she never would. "I refuse to wrestle with the impossible." When Beth was a girl, everyone called her Liz, but after moving from New York to Seattle twenty years ago, she had altered her name to Beth. "New name, new persona, right?" She had never revealed to Gabriel whether she was happier as Beth than she had been as Liz. He supposed she was.

Though Gabriel was in touch with Beth more often than Michael, his encounters with her had also been infrequent over the years. They exchanged Christmas cards, and two years earlier he and Thea had had a drink with her when they passed through Seattle on their way to a trekking vacation in Nepal.

He pictured his sister as he'd seen her then: short black hair shot with white threads, broad forehead, straight nose, squared chin, and slightly protruding teeth that made for a prominent smile—a Fallon face. On Beth, however, the Fallon countenance somehow became pretty. Like almost all Fallons, she was also tall and broad—but not fat. Gabriel considered her striking. And smart. But Beth and he seldom called each other. "I have to talk to you," she'd said on the machine. Clearly something serious had prompted her to reach for him on this afternoon of his nightmare, an accident perhaps or sickness, some financial mess. It was certainly nothing good or she would have spoken of it on the tape. People usually felt obliged to divulge bad news in a more personal way.

Gabriel punched in the number for Beth's studio home. She answered on the second ring, as if she'd been waiting for his call. After an exchange of greetings, she said, "It's about Michael. He has cancer. Of the liver. He's going to die."

Beth's declaration stunned Gabriel. Although he had anticipated some revelation of catastrophe, he had not expected it to center on his brother. Had his nightmare been a premonition?

Beth continued. "Michael went into the hospital last week. Inoperable malignancy. They discharged him last night so he can die at home. Yvonne called me about it this morning, all stressed out. I volunteered to pass the word to you."

Yvonne was Michael's wife. A dry stick of a woman, Gabriel had met her only once, six years ago, on the last occasion he'd seen Michael himself.

To Beth he said, "The diagnosis is certain? Michael's only fifty-two, for Christ's sake."

"He's going to die, Gabe. They sent him home from the hospital to die. It could be a matter of weeks. Nobody's predicting. But it's terminal. Barring a miracle."

Beth fell silent, as if waiting for him to absorb the fact of his brother's impending death. Gabriel imagined her standing in the kitchen of her house, coffee cup in hand, the phone pressed against her ear. Perhaps she was longing for the solace of her darkroom—unable to express her emotions to the elder brother she hardly knew.

Gabriel said, "I ought to call Yvonne."

"Yes, you should. Let me know if there's anything new." They hung up.

Leaning back in his chair, Gabriel looked out to the sun-dappled woods and thought, *My brother is dying.* What am I feeling at this moment? Shock, certainly. All such mortal news shocked the recipient, especially when it came like a mugger out of an alley. But what else was he feeling? Something. Something else.

Gabriel cast his mind back six years to his last meeting with his brother. Michael, who manufactured some kind of valve in his Missouri foundry—and made "damn little money at it" according to a Christmas card from Beth—had come east on business. His then-new bride, Yvonne, whom Gabriel had never met, had accompanied him. Thea and Gabriel had taken the newlyweds to dinner at a restaurant in the city. Gabriel had been astonished at how severely time had treated Michael. His hair had turned ashen. He'd looked brittle. His face—freckled in his youth—seemed a caricature of Fallon features. The brow had become a bony carapace, the nose a hatchet blade, and the jaw a fleshless point. Though younger than Gabriel, Michael had looked much older.

The contrast between Thea and Yvonne had been even more striking. Thea, in her late forties then, had never been conventionally pretty. Her too-generous nose, her wing-like brows, and her moistly sensuous mouth had always barred her from mere prettiness. But the combination of these features with her fall of tawny hair and her graceful body produced an electrifying effect: Thea was beautiful. And to her beauty she added a spirit both gentle and buoyant. That night, in a clinging black dress and radiating vitality, she had compelled admiration from all who beheld her.

On the other hand Yvonne—whom Michael called Vonnie—struck Gabriel as dry. Her face, under its cap of brown hair, was furrowed as if she had labored long years in the sun. Her mouth turned downward, giving her an air of disappointment. Divorced from a hard-luck cattle rancher, she had been Michael's assistant before their marriage. This was her first trip out of Missouri. Though only forty-five, she seemed worn beyond her years. Obviously uncomfortable in the glare of Thea's splendor, she mumbled only an occasional sentence during dinner.

Nor did Gabriel and Michael have much to say to each other. By the time dessert arrived, the brothers had resorted to talking about the Cardinals and Yankees while the women yawned. The two couples had parted before midnight.

When they got home, Thea and Gabriel had made love to exhaustion, as if to defy the dominion of time which had so ravaged Michael and his woman.

Gabriel had not spoken with his brother since that night.

Now the time had come to break the silence. Gabriel stared at the phone. It was possible that Yvonne would receive his overture with hostility, viewing him as the bad brother seeking, too late, a share in her family's mourning. But he had to make the call. He tapped out the number. A tired voice answered. "Vonnie Fallon." Prepared for rebuke, Gabriel identified himself.

She repeated his name as if amazed to hear from him. Then she said, "Beth explained the situation to you?"

Gabriel detected no animosity in her question. "Beth said it was terminal."

"Yes, the doctors tell us it's progressing fairly quickly. You know how they talk: progressing."

As if reciting a text, she went on to say that the medics had declared treatment useless, though they wouldn't estimate how much life Michael might have left. So he'd come home. Given the circumstances, his spirits were good.

All at once Gabriel wanted desperately to speak to his brother for reasons he could not have articulated except to say they had to do with boyhood, estrangement, and above all with the stone of grief that had formed in his throat. He said, "Can I talk to him, Yvonne?"

"Oh sure, Michael has no trouble talking. Seems like that's all we do these days, talk. I'll put him on for you."

Gabriel held the phone against his ear. What would he and his brother say to each other after so much silence? Would Michael express bitterness for Gabriel's neglect of him? Well, he was entitled.

"Gabe, I'm glad to hear from you."

Michael's voice sounded strong. Despite Yvonne's assurances, Gabriel had expected speech slurred by morphine. He said the first words that came to mind. "You sound cheerful, Michael, in spite of the circumstances."

"If I sound cheerful, it's 'cause I'm full of dope." Clearly, with his time running out, Michael did not intend to waste his strength in recriminations. "I guess you know I'm not going to get well again, Gabe. That's the reality. I'm resigned to it, ready for eternity. Still, I'd like to spend a last Christmas with my family."

Gabriel searched his memory for what he knew of Michael's family. There were two sons and a daughter, he recalled—all children by Michael's first wife, Olivia, who died in an auto accident fifteen years ago. The daughter (Mona, wasn't it?) was the firstborn. She and the elder son (Lawrence?) had both gotten married young, and the daughter already had children of her own. The younger son (whose name Gabriel couldn't recollect) had to be about college age by now.

Reverting to Michael's wish to spend a last Christmas with his family, Gabriel said, "You always loved the holidays, Michael, even as a kid."

As if Gabriel's observation had stimulated him, Michael launched into a monologue focused on memories of sledding, skating, swimming, and horsing around in upstate New York where the brothers had spent several years of their boyhood. As Michael chattered, Gabriel reflected on what seemed to him an irony: the town they were referring to was only an hour's drive from where he and Thea now lived in the Catskills town of Margaretville.

Michael said, "We sure had some fun when we were kids, didn't we, Gabe?"

Gabriel agreed that they certainly had, though in fact he couldn't recollect much about those years that he would describe as fun. What he remembered most was the sense of abandonment that had dominated his young life. When he was seven and Michael five, their parents had boarded them with strangers in order to engage in mysterious pursuits of their own. Thus Michael and Gabriel had passed months at a time with a variety of caretakers, not all of them kindly. For Gabriel childhood had been a time of loneliness, of nights spent crying in the dark. But for his brother, evidently, it held some shining memories, and so Gabriel listened without comment until Michael ran out of reminiscences. Then he put to his dying brother a question that was perhaps an attempt to extract some balm for the desolation of his own smashed life. "Are you really ready, Michael? Do you really feel at peace?"

Michael snorted a laugh. "People are always asking me that now. Am I at peace? Do I expect eternal life? The answer is yes to both questions. I'm ready to go because I've accomplished my goal on earth: the education of my kids." Amplifying, he said that his daughter (yes, Mona was her name) had her master's degree. Lawrence was a physician married to another physician. And Peter, the youngest, was heading to graduate school in the fall. "Olivia and I promised each other that, if we accomplished nothing else, we'd see that our kids got all the education they could absorb. So after Olivia died, I made that my ambition. Wasn't easy. Money was always tight. But I was lucky. I got it done. So if I meet Olivia in the hereafter, she'll have no complaints. That'll be a novelty, Olivia not bitching at me."

Gabriel called up an image of Olivia and Michael when they'd been students together at St. John's University in Brooklyn, where each of them had acquired a degree in business. He couldn't imagine pretty Olivia, so unlike Yvonne, bitching at anyone let alone Michael, whom she had appeared to worship.

Michael said, "I lived an ordinary life, Gabe. No grand objectives like yours."

Gabriel thought of confessing that his grand objectives had led him only to a dead end, but he held his tongue. It was Michael's life, Michael's date with eternity they were talking about.

Yvonne came on the line. "Time for medication, Mikey." Agreeing to talk further in a week, the brothers hung up.

Gabriel again looked out the window to the woods beyond. He thought, *This is sorrow, this stone in the throat. This is grief.* Was it possible that it was his own spiritual malignancy that had rendered him so responsive to his brother's physical one?

Confronted with the unanswerable, he went downstairs to find Thea and let her know of Michael's illness. He discovered a note on the kitchen counter: "Gone shopping." Thwarted, he wandered into the living room where, as usual, he experienced an upsurge of loathing not just for the room but for the entire house.

Thea and Gabriel had rented the place in order to test conditions in the Catskills before deciding whether to settle there. But the house soon had begun to repel them. Three stories high, its owner had built it alongside a stream that ran between two forested hills. In every room, floor-to-ceiling windows afforded views of the woods beyond while annihilating any sense of privacy. Too big and too gloomy (despite all the glass), Thea and Gabriel had come to hate the house. But it possessed one attribute that both of them found enchanting: a waterfall.

Called Eternity Falls, this twenty-foot-high avalanche of water roared over a granite crag only thirty yards from the house. Visible from every room, it was a constant presence. It got its name because, according to legend, a ghostly maiden (a kind of rural nymph, Gabriel supposed, though of course he had never glimpsed her) guarded a gate to eternity located in the rock wall behind the falling water. Hence Eternity Falls.

Now, as Gabriel stared at the cascade through the living-room glass, the column of water gleamed like marble in the sunlight. Its thunder echoed throughout the house.

Drawn as he often was by the music of the falls, Gabriel went out and made his way to the bank of the stream. He felt on his face the droplets thrown up by the torrent. Eternity Falls—a fitting place to weigh his brother's assertion that he was ready for whatever eternity awaited him.

How curious, thought Gabriel, *that Michael had described his own life as ordinary but himself as lucky.* Gabriel knew that most people would consider him far more fortunate than his dying brother. Not only was he still whole physically (even the arrhythmia of his heart was more frightening than threatening according to the doctors), he also had the love of the woman he cherished. He was on excellent terms with his adult children. He had prospered at his craft while producing books that (until recent insights) he had considered good work. Thus life had blessed him far above his brother. Yet Michael was at peace in the face of death, while Gabriel was wracked by a torment inexplicable to others, even to Thea—a torment that caused him shame as well as pain.

Staring into the cascade, Gabriel let its ceaselessness lead his mind away. Unexpectedly he found himself retracing his life with Thea, as if he might find in that golden landscape some key to healing his misery—and perhaps saving his life.

CHAPTER 2

FROM THE BEGINNING, DESPITE inevitable disagreements and occasional outbursts of fury, Thea and Gabriel had enjoyed a conspicuous compatibility. And it had been so since their first meeting in New York in the spring of 1964, before Vietnam became the nation's obsession. Gabriel had been only twenty then. Gangling and shy, he had developed the habit of trying to compensate for his shyness with smiles and an eagerness to please.

In that spring Gabriel was already a veteran urbanite. Three years earlier, after graduation from Fordham Prep, a Jesuit secondary school in the Bronx, he had found a job as a copy boy with the *New York Daily News*. He had then fled to Manhattan, where he shared a studio in Chelsea with three other *News* copy boys.

Soon, having passed his apprenticeship as a fetcher of coffee and booze for the needy of the City Room, he'd been assigned to man the editorial switchboard during the day shift—the slowest news hours for a morning paper. His elevation from the copy boy ranks added just enough to his salary to allow him to enroll in night classes at NYU, where he took courses in English literature, classical history, and the modern novel.

For the next two years Gabriel went to school by night and worked the dayside at the *News*. He also pursued what he called life; that is, he fell in with a coterie of young men and women much like himself who drank in Village bars, smoked pot in coffeehouses, and espoused what they termed (with monumental naïveté) revolutionary upheaval. Gabriel and his companions also wrangled over art, poetry, philosophy, and the meaning of the universe—all to the wail of folk songs. Thus he lived happily in a chaos of music, art, talk, drink, marijuana, laughter, and of course, sex.

Gabriel, however, proved a slow starter in the sex sweepstakes. Though attractive to girls, he often became too wrapped in the rhetoric of the day to recognize when to stop talking and instead carpe the sexual diem. As a result he consummated few sexual encounters with the self-proclaimed radical girls of his circle, and he managed to achieve only one ongoing liaison. The girl, a junior editor at MacMillan, ended the affair by going home to Wisconsin to marry a lawyer. Her defection had crushed Gabriel—briefly.

After two years of manning phones and filling in at "rewrite" whenever a staffer failed to show for work, Gabriel, whose willingness had made him a favorite of the City Editor, was advanced—despite his youth—to reporter. Assigned to Manhattan police headquarters at Center Street, his duty there was to monitor the police radio and call in anything that sounded newsworthy. The job soon bored him. Most of the time he sat around, one ear cocked to the radio, and played hearts. But he consoled himself with the knowledge that he was finally making a salary he could live on.

Thus he soon moved out of his shared quarters in Chelsea into what New Yorkers called a garden apartment—a combination living room, bedroom, and kitchen area. It was located on the ground-floor rear of a brownstone on West Seventy-First Street, around the corner from the canopies and doormen of Central Park West. The garden part of the apartment consisted of a patch of earth outside his back door.

His new digs provided Gabriel with the privacy he craved to come and go, entertain, and above all, write. This was the secret that he had harbored since boyhood. He wanted to write. The written word entranced him. These marks on paper, senseless in themselves, fascinated him with their capacity to link minds, evoke the senses, and transmit ideas. Moreover, the same marks called forth different sights and sounds in each mind they entered. The written word was a mystery that Gabriel had to master.

Thus it had become his life's purpose to make himself a writer, a serious writer, not just a hack like the rewrite guys at the *News,* who would boast of the yarns they were working on or the war stories they would pour out when they had the time.

Over years of reading and experimentation with words on the page, Gabriel had developed his own conception of what it meant to be a serious writer. Serious writers knew how to create life. They possessed the power to bring into existence for readers a world not their own, but one made their own by words on paper. That was Gabriel's hunger: to make worlds with words.

He had revealed none of this to anyone, not even to his poet-friend Jeremy Halperin, who was eight years older than he and also a reporter at the *News.* Although Gabriel considered Jeremy a buddy, he had hidden his ambition from him, not only because he feared to seem pretentious in Jeremy's eyes but also because intuition warned him that he could only gain the prize he sought by private struggle. Thus, maintaining silence about his goal, he moved into the garden apartment on West Seventy-First Street to begin pursuing his vision.

It was there that he met Thea. The details of that meeting remained ever afterward woven into Gabriel's memory like music that never failed to move. In later years he needed only to close his eyes and focus to re-experience that first encounter.

It took place on a Saturday afternoon in March, two days after Gabriel had settled into his new quarters. He went out into the hallway to get his mail and found a young woman there. Barefoot, clad in white short-shorts and a blue T-shirt, she was sweeping the carpet before the door of the only other apartment on the ground floor, the one that fronted the street. Realizing that she was his neighbor, Gabriel considered introducing himself, but the young woman seemed intent on her task, as unwilling to look up and catch his eye as he was to stand mute and gape at her. And so, choosing the classic New York resolution of an awkward moment, he moved to go past her to the mailboxes without acknowledging her presence. As he did so he heard her say in a low voice, "Don't step in the derbis."

Not sure he'd heard her correctly, he halted. "The what?"

"The derbis." She pointed to the pile of dust she had accumulated. "Okay, the *debris* then. Just a little humor there. Eases the tension between strangers, right?"

He smiled. "Oh, I see." He wanted to make a playful remark of his own to show her that he wasn't as stupid as he probably seemed, but he couldn't think of anything the least bit clever to say.

She said, "I'm Thea. Marek. I live here." She indicated the closed door of her apartment. "My roommate and I. She's a stew. Never home. I'm a dancer. Out of work. Home a lot."

Gabriel reciprocated by giving her his name and the fact that he worked for the *News*.

"Oh, a reporter! Great! Can you get my picture in the paper?"

"Only if you commit a crime. I'm a police reporter."

"Okay, how about this? I put on my leotards and pretend to rob a bank. You could write the story, 'Desperate Dancer Foiled in Bank Heist.' In the photos I'll look contrite but sexy. I have great legs, if you haven't noticed. What do you say? I'm out of work at the moment. I could use the publicity."

Thea's good humor made Gabriel smile. He said, "You'd get lots of publicity all right. The trouble is you might have to spend some time behind bars, even for a fake heist. Very unpleasant. Not much help for your career there."

"Yeah, I didn't think of that. Okay. Erase the desperate-dancer idea."

She unleashed a hearty laugh. For the first time Gabriel perceived Thea's unorthodox beauty: a smile like a sunrise, moistly sensuous lips, gull-wing brows shading eyes that seemed to glow with their own blue light—all this framed by lion-colored hair falling around an oval face that was not at all pretty but enchanting in its oddity. And if her face was lovely, her body—displayed in the shorts and T-shirt—was superb: neat ankles, long, powerful dancer's legs, curving hips, a narrow waist, delicate pointed breasts, and a columnar neck surmounted by that face.

Thea also seemed to radiate warmth and light, as if her body contained some incandescent source of energy. It made Gabriel edge closer to her, the better to experience the pull of that inner glow. He found himself wondering what it would be like to hold her against him. A moment later he astonished himself with the realization that he wanted to love her; he wanted her to love him. Astounding himself still further, he said, "You take my breath away." She laughed. But both of them later agreed that their life together began with those words.

For their first date Gabriel and Thea took the subway to Coney Island. Thea wore white sandals and a miniskirt that showed to advantage her tanned legs. At Coney they rode the Wonder Wheel and the Cyclone, and Thea supplied screams of feigned fright that invited Gabriel to hold her body against his. He could do nothing wrong that night. He won every arcade game he played. By the time they left for home, Thea's arms were overflowing with stuffed animals, souvenir replicas of the Empire State Building, ceramic ashtrays, and even a bowl of live goldfish—so much silly loot that Thea gave away most of it to passersby, retaining only a cockeyed panda for herself. "Because I think he really loves me." Coming back on the train, Gabriel kissed her. Later, in his apartment, they made love.

After this they spent hours—and then days—together. It seemed to both of them that they never stopped talking, revealing themselves. Gabriel learned that she was nineteen, an orphan, raised in institutions and foster homes. She had made her way alone in the world. Somehow she had evaded the self-pity she might have embraced given the cards fate had dealt to her. Instead she had made herself joyful, loving, and self-assured. Never had Gabriel felt so at ease in the company of another. She earned her living as a chorus-line gypsy, trooping from show to show as needed. She said she loved being a dancer, not because she dreamed of stardom but because the art itself moved her with its physical precision. Whenever Gabriel watched her perform, her pleasure in the performance enthralled him.

In bed Thea was passionate, tender, unembarrassed by fantasy. She enchanted him.

One night, mad with love for her, Gabriel dared to confess his hunger to make himself a serious writer. Her reaction sent him soaring with joy because it meant that she understood the force of his need: "You want to be like God. You want to make worlds. Didn't God use words to fill his nothing?"

She was perfection.

Gabriel began to think of Thea as his own goddess. Within weeks of meeting her, convinced that he would never find another so good and beautiful, he suggested they get married. She said, "Or we could live together. We are kind of young for marriage."

But it was marriage he wanted, certification of what they had discovered in each other. He said, "Don't you want to marry me?"

"Yes, I do." She laughed at her choice of words. "I do."

Gabriel's friend Jeremy warned him against it. "Don't marry Thea if you intend to do anything with your life. You're just kids. The two of you will run aground. But even if you don't, she's too fucking good. She'll spoil your nose for the rottenness of this world. She'll make you happy. She'll be fatal to any talent you might possess."

But they married, and they found they were happy. Luckily Gabriel escaped the war. He and Thea had children, Richard and Valerie, and moved to a suburb in New Jersey. Gabriel lost touch with Jeremy and with other friends in the city. He and Thea joined protests against the war. They traveled together in Europe.

For a while, caught up in the zeitgeist of the seventies, they flung themselves into sexual experimentation that involved role-playing fantasy, multiple partners, and exotic forms of lovemaking. But in the end these explorations only demonstrated that they thrilled each other above all lesser thrills.

In time Thea, missing the art she loved and had left behind in the city, opened a dance school in their community.

Meanwhile, Gabriel earned a living as a reporter and then as a columnist for a suburban newspaper. Eventually needing to add income for a house, tuition, and the orthodontist, he forsook journalism to produce commercial video—an occupation that, to his surprise, he thoroughly enjoyed. During this period he also turned out two novels set in seventeenth-century Ireland and two histories on the slave trade and Elizabethan sea voyages. His books enjoyed moderate success and he thought them good. But he knew they were not the work of a serious writer.

The day arrived when Gabriel realized that time had turned against him. If he were ever to become the writer he yearned to be, he would have to consecrate himself to achieving his life's purpose.

Thus, in their middle years, Thea and Gabriel decided to seek a kind of rebirth in the Catskill Mountains of New York. They had shared a life of passion in sex, travel, and community service. They had done more than most. Their children were grown. It was time to embark on a new adventure.

Thea, eager to embrace whatever destiny offered, was overjoyed by the prospect. It would give her an opportunity to try her hand at composing a memoir of her years in a Brooklyn orphanage. "And I can also bake, and read, and jog in the clean air. What else could I possibly want?"

Gabriel, who had spent much of an unhappy boyhood in the Catskills, nevertheless viewed the move there as something of a homecoming, for he retained sweet memories of the countryside, recollecting pastures buzzing with bees and nights so starry you felt you could pluck galaxies from the sky. In the Catskills, Gabriel intended to write a novel he had been contemplating for years: a fantasy that would achieve the excellence he craved. This story, he was sure, would establish him as a serious writer. Yes. And when he wasn't working, he and Thea would walk in the woods. They would read and talk away the evenings. Thus, expecting joy, Thea and Gabriel rented the Eternity Falls house and moved in.

Two days later, on the night of the October full moon, Gabriel went out to stand by the falls. The disk of the moon had just lifted above the hills. Winter was already breathing over the Catskills. Crystals of ice clung to the base of the cataract. Staring up at the spread of stars, Gabriel experienced the sensation of rising into the stellar cold. Then one of the stars began to move across the heavens. A drone pierced the night. What Gabriel had taken for a star was an airplane invading the dark. His heart filled with rage against this aggression.

That incident proved to be only the beginning. Thea and Gabriel soon learned that noise intruded everywhere in the countryside. Trucks loaded with tree trunks rumbled along the road. Squadrons of all-terrain vehicles, manned by eleven-year-olds and their fathers, trespassed in the woods. The days resounded with the crack of rifles and the whine of chain saws. Packs of drunken snowmobilers trashed the trails. The helicopters of the drug police clattered overhead in search of marijuana plantations.

Clearly Thea and Gabriel were not to find their paradise in the Catskills. Curiously, however, they found they were able to work well—perhaps in compensation for their disappointment otherwise.

Thea labored every day on her memoir. Gabriel's novel flowed from his imagination. In the narrative, a poet travels to a primitive world where he becomes a heroic adventurer. In the end the hero casts off his humanity and morphs into a vagabond spirit in space. Gabriel called his tale *Avernus,* after his invented world. As the story came alive, he soared with confidence. He considered *Avernus* his best work—an original vision superior to anything he'd ever done before.

Gabriel completed *Avernus* in six months while the snow clung to the hemlocks and Eternity Falls rumbled behind a wall of ice. Jubilant that he had finally created a serious work but in need of confirmation, he sent copies of the manuscript to friends whose opinions he respected.

Their reaction shocked him. Instead of the praise he had anticipated, he detected, behind the gentility of language, a unanimous judgment: *Avernus* was a failure. In a frenzy of disbelief, Gabriel reread the manuscript. To his horror, he now found the tale a pretentious miscarriage. It rang like a cracked bell. *Avernus* was junk.

The realization panicked Gabriel. Had he overvalued his gift all these years?

Despite his dread of what he might bring to light, he forced himself to revisit his previous work. He found his books all well-constructed, even intelligent. Why not? He was a professional after all. He knew how to churn out prose for publication. But the truth confronted him on every page: junk. Where he had meant to create authenticity, he had fabricated falsity.

This recognition evoked in him emotions reminiscent of those he'd felt as a boy when his feckless parents had left him and his brother with strangers: a sense of worthlessness and rage. He was not a serious writer after all. He was a contriver. He had deluded himself that he was like a bird in a cage, that one day the door would open and he would fly. But now he saw that he would never fly, that he had been a flightless bird all along. Nothing could compensate for that, not Thea's love, not all the lesser achievements of his life. His heart lay smashed.

Despair took root in Gabriel like a malignancy. As if wading in a swamp of self-pity and grief, he spent hours wandering about the house. Sometimes, to Thea's alarm, he would erupt in crying jags. He was a flightless bird and had consumed his only life trying to reach the unattainable sky. The crying jags brought him no surcease either. And when the tears dried up, he sought respite in booze.

All the time, however, he was well aware that his crackup had no meaning for anyone but him. The world didn't care that he had failed, and why should it care? Often he felt disgust for the self-pity that engulfed him, but he could find no cure for it. He had become a man who hated what he was.

As the blackness thickened in his soul, Gabriel's heart began to beat irregularly as if to underscore the brevity of the time left to him. He came to regard the erratic thumping under his ribs as the physical manifestation of his broken spirit.

Though sympathetic to Gabriel's darkness, Thea confessed that she was unable to comprehend it. She implored him to visit a psychiatrist. He refused without explanation. Frustrated, she railed at his refusal calling it an act of aggression against her. "Why do you want to hurt me? You have talent, Gabe. You know that! You have people who love you. You have me, goddamn it! Let me help you!" His drinking frightened her too. "Who knows what you might do when you're drunk? Can't you see that drowning yourself in alcohol is just a form of self-indulgence?" But Gabriel remained impervious.

In reality it was not self-indulgence but shame that sealed him inside his desolation. In a world where innocents perished in agony every day, how could he justify his misery even to Thea? Even to himself? He also recognized that his torment was far from unique. It was epidemic among all those who woke one day to recognition of failure after a lifetime's striving. Plumbers, politicians, engineers, farmers, teachers, cops—no one was immune. Most people ended up as distortions of whatever they once wished to be. The world was crawling with tarnished beauties, neglected poets, drunken doctors, and lost dreamers. He was just another of that brokenhearted legion. But this awareness changed nothing. His heart lay shattered. No doctor could repair it.

As Gabriel's melancholia deepened, a derisive refrain began to sound in his head at unpredictable times. It might begin while he was taking a shower or walking to the mailbox: *You wasted your life. You wasted your life. Wasted your life. Like a piss in the ocean.*

It sounded like a child's teasing and it was somehow familiar, though Gabriel could not identify its jeering cadence. *You wasted your life. Like a piss in the ocean.*

With the onset of the taunting, the darkest of thoughts began to slither about in his brain. Since he now realized he couldn't write, did he want to live? He knew that Thea would be terrified if she ever heard him voice that question, and so he kept it to himself. Nor did he tell her of the singsong teasing in his head. But in the sleepless nights it throbbed in his mind. *You wasted your life. Like a piss in the ocean.*

Sometimes the taunting took another tack: Whine. Whine. Whine. It's unworthy. He agreed with the voice but felt powerless to stem the tide of self-pity engulfing him.

The arrival of the Catskill spring brought no improvement in his state. His drinking continued as if he intended to blot out any suggestion of nature's benevolence. But booze could not blot out Eternity Falls. Thus, when weather permitted and he was sober enough to do so, Gabriel took to going to the waterfall, where he would stand transfixed as the water plunged from now to then—rather like existence itself.

To his astonishment the pounding of the cataract seemed to provide a temporary anodyne to his misery—so much so that the roaring of the falls could sometimes obviate even his desire for whiskey. And so, by degrees, it had become his custom to visit the falls daily, often for hours at a time.

Accordingly, on the afternoon he learned of his brother's illness, Gabriel took himself to the falls in order to gnaw over Michael's claim that he was at peace in the face of death. Could that be true? Was Michael's peace a natural mercy, a descent of grace at the end, or only self-deception? And did it matter? Gabriel thought too of the paradox he saw in his brother's pending death: while Michael would certainly choose to extend his life if he could do so, Gabriel was contemplating an intentional end to his.

As he sought to get his mind around these matters, Gabriel gradually became aware of what sounded like indistinct words in the cataract's thunder before him. A repetitive phrase seemed to be issuing from the torrent itself. The voice of the girl guardian of the gate behind the water? Ridiculous. Still he found the phenomenon impossible to ignore, though he knew its source might lie in his head, a residue of too much booze in recent weeks rather than the falling water. Thus he strained to make sense of the sounds. But it proved impossible. As with a voice calling from a distance, he could detect the tantalizing words, if words they were, in the roar but could not decipher them. And then another sound interfered: the Jeep.

Thea had returned from Margaretville. Whatever Gabriel might have heard in the waterfall, it was gone now. In any case he had more on his mind than some aural illusion. Turning away from the waterfall, he went to inform Thea that his brother was dying.

CHAPTER 3

GABRIEL FOUND THEA IN the kitchen. Bags of groceries lay on the counters. In her white shorts, sky-blue tank top, and white sandals, with her blonde mane hanging loose, she looked preternaturally youthful, as if immune to the penalties of time.

Gabriel poured himself a Scotch and began telling her about Michael, even reconstructing their phone conversation. When he finished, she threw her arms around him. Then, stepping back, she gripped his upper arms and speared him with her eyes. "As terrible as it is, Michael's sickness is a warning to you, Gabe. Live now. Stop grieving for yourself. Grieve for Michael if you must grieve. His life is really over."

Gabriel couldn't help but smile at her vehemence. She was even using the news about Michael to combat the sickness that was sucking the life from her husband. Still clinging to Gabriel, she said, "Think of the good things you have, Gabe. Think about the kids being here."

This was a reference to a visit from Richard and his family, who would be coming from Chicago to stay for a week around the Fourth of July holiday. Valerie, taking a break from her studies, was supposed to join them as well. Thea hoped that this gathering, which she anticipated with joy, might dispel Gabriel's darkness. He knew better. But he wouldn't mar her hope by saying so.

Removing her hold on his arms, Thea began putting cans and boxes into cabinets. Gabriel finished his Scotch and joined her. As they worked, she said, "It's strange that you and Michael shared the same awful childhood, yet he recalls it fondly and you never even want to talk about it."

"Not odd. Michael's tinting his memory with rose. Besides it was more than forty years ago."

"People never forget those early years."

Preferring as always to avoid discussion of his childhood, Gabriel reverted to a theme that usually fended off such talk. "The past is past, Thea. Everybody has a rotten childhood one way or another, and so what? There's no use crying over it."

But she wouldn't let go. "Granted. But everybody's got to make peace with that part of themselves. It seems that Michael's done it. Why haven't you, Gabe?"

This was a question she'd been putting to him off and on since the beginning of their life together. Gabriel answered it as he always did: "I buried my childhood shit long ago."

As always, Thea shot him a skeptical glance as if to say, "Hey, Gabe, don't kid me. I was an orphan. Nobody can bury that shit."

Gabriel ignored her challenge. Even Thea couldn't goad him into talking about all that. In silence they continued stashing the groceries. As they did so, Gabriel allowed his thoughts to drift back to Woodstock, an indulgence he seldom permitted himself.

He had to admit that, like Michael, he could recollect some of those Woodstock times with a smile. But what he remembered most about the boyhood he had shared with Michael—more than a decade before the birth of their sister, Beth—was the conviction instilled in him then that he must have committed some wickedness that caused his parents to abandon him to strangers. Or maybe he just wasn't worth keeping.

Thea's incredulity notwithstanding, Gabriel was satisfied that he had long ago come to terms with the pain inflicted on his boy-self. As a young man living on his own, he had forced himself to examine his memories of his parents in an attempt to see them as they really had been. Though, admittedly, he had viewed them through the lens of childhood recollection, he felt sure that he had taken an accurate fix in concluding that his mother and father, both of them selfish and ignorant, had lacked the capacity to sense the suffering of others. Accordingly, they never scrupled to employ any cruelty on anybody, including their children, to further their ends.

Thus, heedlessly, they had crippled their sons not through physical abuse or malnutrition but through casual acts of scorn, indifference, and neglect, which, though never making headlines, are most effective in turning kids into impaired adults. His parents' neglect, born of self-absorption, their indifference to censure, their readiness to play at affection—offering and then withholding it—had planted in Gabriel and, to a lesser degree in Michael, a sense of guilt and worthlessness that carried over into adulthood.

Gabriel had never been able to determine just why his parents had acted as they did—or what made them the monsters they were. He knew he would never solve that part of their mystery, but he felt confident that, for the most part, he had long ago unraveled the enigma of their destructive behavior. And having perceived as much, he had pushed rancor from his mind and buried his childhood shit in a kind of psychic cave. He had also detached himself from reminders of that past, though doing so had meant separating himself from his brother and his sister. For the same reason, they had done the same. Thea might scoff, but he had made peace with his ghosts in his own way.

As these reflections wound through Gabriel's mind, it dawned on him that the road he had seen in his nightmare that afternoon, the road where the dream car had exploded, was a real place: a country lane somewhere around Woodstock. He could not recall exactly where it had been, but he was certain that he and Michael had walked that road as children. Along with this memory came an intuition that disquieted him: in the days ahead, Michael's journey toward death might arouse emotions in Gabriel that could unseal the psychic cave into which he had dumped the toxic waste of his boyhood. He couldn't allow that. Thus he resolved that if Michael again invoked their childhood when they talked on the phone, he would listen with sympathy, maybe even offer some comment, but he would not allow himself to feel the poison of the past. His childhood shit was going to stay buried. To mark his resolve, Gabriel poured another shot of Chivas.

Silent, eyes closed, Thea lay naked and at peace in Gabriel's arms. Twilight flooded through the bedroom window. It cast a veneer of gold over her ivory skin and spread-out hair. He could hear the rush of the waterfall outside.

They had come up to the bedroom to make love for the first time in several days—a long gap for them. They were engaged in a ritual that pleased both of them: going to bed about seven in the evening light, making love slowly, and then rising to have dinner together.

As the passion flowed between them, Gabriel envisioned an afternoon they had spent in Venice in a hotel overlooking the Grand Canal. The light in that room had quivered with reflections from the canal. The bells of San Marco had been sounding. Whispering endearments, Thea had posed in a flood of gold and undressed for Gabriel as he watched from the bed. Then, as the light bathed her body, he had embraced her. *"Bellina mia."*

Now locked together, Gabriel heard Thea breathing in time with the falling water outside. He drifted off to sleep.

Gabriel hovers above a familiar Woodstock road. Once more he beholds the boy who was him and the boy who was Michael. Dressed alike in navy-blue shorts, sandals, and starched white shirts, the boys are standing together at the edge of the dusty road. It is a hot day. The sun is shedding a harsh light. Gabriel senses that this time, instead of fragmented images, there will be clarity, memory, and truth.

He is within the boy who was young Gabe. He is that boy. He feels the sun as a weight pressing down on the top of his head. Pebbles are glistening in the dust at his feet. He is aware of a lawn behind him. Also behind him on a hill is a white house with a porch and swings and bushes with flowers like snowballs. They have taken him and Michael to this place. Young Gabe and his brother have never seen it before. Young Gabe does not know where he is.

When he looks across to the opposite side of the road, he sees woods filled with trees like Christmas trees. He thinks how cool it must be in those woods. He thinks that in those woods he could cry and no one would forbid it. But here, in the fierce light, he knows he mustn't cry. He brushes the hair from his forehead, a gesture intended to fight back the tears that keep ascending into his eyes from some place inside him.

Young Gabe steals a glance to his left at his chunky, dark-haired brother. He takes Michael's hand in his. She always says, "Take care of your little brother."

Directly before him, blocking out part of the woods on the other side of the road, allowing only the tops of the Christmas trees to show over its roof, is the car. It is blue like the sky. A diamond of light glares where the sun strikes the paint. Young Gabe has to blink when he looks at this diamond of light flaring before him. He tells himself that if he puts out his hand, the one not holding Michael's, and touches the car, the metal will be hot enough to burn him.

They are in the car in the front seat. This time they are not figures wrapped in black but them as they truly were. They are looking out the rolled-down window, looking down at Michael and young Gabe standing together at the side of the road with the lawn and the house behind them.

He is at the steering wheel, on the far side of the car, away from young Gabe and Michael. He is wearing a white shirt and a tie but not a jacket. He likes to wear a jacket. But today it is too hot. He is not smiling. He makes his eyes into slits as if the brightness of the day hurts them even inside the car. His hair is slicked down the way he likes it. Young Gabe can tell that he is in a hurry to start the car and be away.

She is also in the front seat. She is looking out the window nearest to her boys. Young Gabe sees that she has made herself pretty today, excited because this is a day of getting away. She has piled her long hair the color of chestnuts on her head. It's the way she likes her hair when the day is hot. She is wearing a white dress with blue buttons up the front, and white gloves. A white purse too. She has the purse in her hand. She leans out the window. She says, "Kiss me good-bye."

Pulling Michael with him, young Gabe steps up to the window. He touches his lips to the cheek she turns to him. Her skin is slippery with powder that tastes bitter. Michael kisses her too. Young Gabe tells himself again that he mustn't cry. They don't like it if he cries when they go away. She smiles. Her lipstick looks wet. She says, "Now you take care of Michael, Gabriel. Okay?" He nods. He mustn't cry.

The car starts. It vibrates before him. He stares at the blue fog of gas smell that now hangs in the sunlight. The smell turns his stomach. He mustn't vomit either.

He hears his heart beating in his ears now. He knows they will soon be gone. He doesn't want them to go. He doesn't know where he is. He would like to ask where he is. He would also like to ask when they are coming back, if they are coming back, and why they are going in the first place. But he says nothing. They don't like it if he asks questions. He blinks to keep the tears back.

Now young Gabe realizes that the male is saying something from the far side. Holding on to the wheel, he is calling out the window over the rumble of the car. "You fellows have fun, okay?"

Young Gabe nods. So does Michael.

The car lurches forward. As it rolls away the boys can see her hand waving out the window. White gloves. She calls out a single word: "Bye."

Taking Michael by the wrist now, as if to assure himself that his brother at least will remain with him, young Gabe watches as the car gains speed. He wills it to stop, but nothing happens. The car disappears around a curve, leaving a cloud of dust behind it.

He watches the dust hang in the air. Maybe if he wishes hard, they will come back. Maybe they will take him and Michael to wherever it is they are going.

He prays to God, though he is not sure who God is, where he is, or if he cares. "Please God let them come back before the dust is gone."

But the dust settles back onto the road and they don't come back. They won't come back because they don't love him and Michael. He grinds his teeth and prays for God to make the car explode and burn with them in it. But he knows it won't happen. God doesn't love him either.

He feels a hand on the back of his neck. He shivers. It is a man's hand, the hand of the stranger who now controls him. Obediently, with Michael in tow, Gabe lets the hand turn him away from the dirt road and toward the house where he and Michael will now live.

At last he cries.

Ashamed of the tears that feel hot on his cheeks, Gabe squeezes Michael's wrist, as if that act can shut off the tears. Michael says, "It's okay, Gabe."

Young Gabe flies into a fury at his little brother. "Shut up! You just shut up!"

The man's voice says, "All right, boys, that's enough."

They start toward the house.

Suddenly, at an upstairs window, young Gabe sees another boy, one dressed exactly like him and Michael, the same age as young Gabe but with dark skin. The boy in the window has a crippled right arm from which dangles a shrunken hand with a fringe of shriveled fingers. Young Gabe knows that the boy is a victim of polio. The boy at the window smiles and waves his arm, flapping the fingers as if in greeting. He seems to know young Gabe though they have never laid eyes on each other before.

Neither Michael nor their adult keeper notices the crippled boy in the window. It's as if for them he doesn't exist. Then, in the way of dreams, young Gabe knows that the other boy is called Toby Myers, and that he and Toby Myers will be friends. But they might become enemies as well, for there is something mean in the eyes of Toby Myers.

Gasping for breath, Gabriel woke. His heart was flopping under his ribs. His head ached from the Scotch he'd downed before going to bed. Though he'd been sleeping naked, he was soaked in sweat. He felt the dream-boy's tears in his eyes.

The clock on Thea's dresser indicated that it was just past three a.m. A moonless night hid the woods outside the bedroom window. Thea, who also slept naked, lay at his side, every limb relaxed. She would lie that way until, as always, she woke at five a.m. to begin her day. Gabriel marveled at her ability to slumber in peace in spite of any stresses in her life.

28

His heart slowing, he lay on his back and stared into the darkness to reflect on the nightmare that had awakened him. Unlike his dream of the black-clad giants, this one had been more a vision of the past, more memory than nightmare. It had depicted what really happened on that road four decades ago—a scene his giant dream had cloaked in imagery.

This latest nightmare had even set forth young Gabe's first encounter with Toby Myers, a being that only young Gabe ever saw or heard, a being who was at various times young Gabe's companion, advisor, and tormentor, and always his secret.

For the first time in many years, Gabriel found himself contemplating Toby Myers, who had played such an important part in his childhood. Of course, from his first appearance in the window, young Gabe had accepted the presence of Toby Myers in his life. How could he have done otherwise? Hadn't Toby been visible and audible to him, if to no one else?

Only when young Gabe entered the storm of puberty had Toby Myers begun to fade from his mind. And only in adolescence had the maturing Gabriel recognized Toby as the kind of imaginary playmate that lonely children frequently invent, though Toby had often behaved less pleasantly than most such figments.

Later, as an adult, Gabriel had occasionally thought back on the invented companion of his boyhood and wondered if he had modeled his Toby after some real Toby Myers long lost to his memory. But if Toby had ever existed as anything other than young Gabe's fanciful comrade, Gabriel had forgotten the fact.

Eventually Gabriel had dismissed Toby as a childhood doppelganger of sorts and buried him along with his other childhood shit. But now, it seemed, his fabricated playmate and sometime doppelganger had resurfaced in the dream—exactly as young Gabe had experienced him.

With a start of recognition that sent a tremor through his body, it now came to Gabriel that it was almost certainly the child voice of Toby Myers that he'd been hearing jeering in his head: *You wasted your life. Like a piss in the ocean.* Obviously, despite his resolve to keep the past entombed, Gabriel had allowed Michael's approaching death to tear open the cave where he had immured such childhood shit.

Once more Gabriel pictured the two boys standing hand in hand on the road. Once more the car, which he now identified as his father's Nash Rambler, drove away in a whirl of dust. Again the tears threatened. Again Toby waved his withered right arm from the window. Gabriel hadn't revisited that road or that first encounter with Toby for decades. There could be no doubt of it: The shit was washing from the earth. The dead were rising. That past had to be reinterred, but how was Gabriel to accomplish the task? For once booze did not seem the answer. Instead Gabriel's writer's instinct told him to rebury the past beneath a mound of words.

Knowing that he wouldn't sleep again that night, Gabriel got out of bed without disturbing Thea. He pulled on jeans and a T-shirt. Barefoot, he made his way to the study. There on the desk he found a half-filled old notebook, one he had used for constructing his mental picture of the *Avernus* fantasy world. He opened it to the blank pages toward the back of the book. He began to write with a ballpoint pen. He set down the words as they came, without regard for their rhythm or the logic of their progression. After all, he did not intend his words for any reader but only as a way to return the dead to their graves by restating judgments he had already made of them. He wrote:

> My strange, unfeeling parents always seemed to be locked together in combat, as if hate was the force that bound them together. They thought themselves the center of the world, and they could not see beyond themselves. Why were they as they were? I shall never know. I have only scant knowledge of their own peculiar histories since they were as secretive as they were selfish. But there are hints to be found in the little I have managed to scrape together about them.
>
> My father grew up wild in New York City, the youngest son of a misanthropic police detective. His mother died when he was only five. In effect, since his father paid him little attention, he was raised by four much older brothers whose primary ambitions were to cow the world about them, to bend it to their will by any

method available. I don't mean that they were criminals. No. But they were all cheats and cynics living just inside the law. They believed in stripping the other guy before he stripped you. To them a lie was merely a means to an end.

These are truths I learned in retrospect from various sources over the years, including my own later experience of my father's brothers when they were old men.

My father came to manhood believing the world a racket and the population composed of suckers and wise guys who preyed on them. Among the wise guys, he counted himself. He cultivated contempt for anyone not "in the know," as he often phrased it. He thought himself clever, pretending to be educated though he wasn't and pretending to have read books he'd never even looked at. In fact, he was a con man and not a particularly talented one. He once worked in a carnival. Outside of that, as far as I know, he never had a real job. He always spoke of himself as a "speculator." He always had "projects underway." One of his projects, as I recall, involved the marketing of "cushion-soft toilet seats." It never got off the ground. He claimed that he had once been employed as a "collector" for Anthony Anastasia, a big-time mobster who operated on the Brooklyn waterfront in the 1950s. He admired gangsters. He wanted people to think him one. In pursuit of this image, he affected a cool George Raft look: natty suits, a fedora hat, and slicked-back hair. He imagined himself handsome in such getups.

If I know little of my father's true history as opposed to the lies he told about himself, I know even less of my mother's. She never spoke of herself, except to complain of her lot in life. Nor would my chronically ill grandfather, her father whom I came to know a little, say much about her. Her own mother was long dead. I can testify, however, that my mother was pretty, on the verge of beautiful. She had a slender figure. Her face, surrounded by long brown curls, gave off rays of innocence. I can state further that she was the only child of an Irish immigrant who'd risen to some prominence in the New York City construction trades. She'd had a spoiled little girl's upbringing that taught her she was all that counted in the universe. Such savage concentration on herself had hardened her heart to the exclusion of almost all humans. And she was dumb, dumb, dumb, though she, like my father, thought herself highly intelligent. She also thought herself genteel, as she put it, worthy of the best the world had to offer.

As a child, of course, I knew none of this. These were things I learned about my mother and father as I got older. When Michael and I shared a childhood, they were a mystery to me, these parents who told us they loved us and then abandoned us to strangers.

Abandoned us.

There is no other way to put it. They boarded us on farms in villages in upstate New York in homes swarming with blank-eyed foster children. They always left us with strangers, who not only didn't love us, but most of them didn't even like us.

My mother and father would disappear, sometimes for months. We wouldn't know where they were, whether they were ever coming back. No calls, no letters. They forgot us. Michael and I were functional orphans. Worse, we were children who felt ourselves thrown away by parents we both loved and hated.

Sooner or later my mother and father would stop paying for our room and board. The people boarding us would complain, and then grow hostile. Then, apparently after our parents made some kind of settlement, Michael and I would be passed on to some other place.

Sometimes this move would occur after a brief, hope-filled reunion with our parents, but more often than not the new people would merely pick us up in their car and transfer us to our new quarters. We must have stayed with eight different families over a five-year period. It was all terribly confusing, terribly wrenching.

In defense against the loneliness, I made up a friend and for some reason called him Toby Myers. So real did he become to me that I could see him as clearly as I saw my brother, Michael. Toby and I talked together, played together, and sometimes fought as well. Of course I meant Toby Myers to be my friend, my warm pal, but he was more than that. Perhaps, in retrospect, he was often a barometer of my own self-hatred. But this is not the place to analyze the phenomenon of my hallucinatory boyhood playmate.

Why did my mother and father not want Michael and me? Why did they treat us as they did? They never really explained. They would murmur vaguely about having to travel, having to be away to start a new business, having to find a place where all of us could live together. Toby, of course, had a different answer: They just didn't love us, or at least they didn't love me because I was stupid.

In time, from off-hand remarks overheard from uncles and aunts whom I hardly knew, I managed to piece together a confused picture of my mother and father's relationship. It seems that they were constantly engaged in some hideous domestic war. Michael and I were both the pawns and the casualties of their struggle. They sent us away because they were getting a divorce and it was best that we not be with them. Or they sent us away because they were reconciling again and needed to be alone to work things out as they put it. Or my father had to travel, or he was engaged in some get-rich-quick scheme in which children could play no part. Or my father was drinking heavily and my mother had broken down as a consequence. Once I overheard my Uncle Will, one of my father's brothers, remark that my father had cheated a gangster he worked for and that he had to run away and hide. Another time I heard my Aunt Louise grumble that my father had taken money from her and disappeared.

But none of this made sense to me. I could think of only one real reason why they shunted us off to strangers: we were not worthy; we were unlovable. We were being punished for what we were. I never heard a sincere word of love from my parents or from any of those we stayed with. I don't recall my mother ever hugging me or expressing a word of comfort or genuine affection toward me.

I do recall that once, during one of those brief illusory reunions with my parents, my mother, moved by alcohol or some transient emotion, came into the bedroom where my brother and I slept and whispered into our hungry hearts: "I love my sweet angels." But the next day, hung over, she peevishly lamented to us that we were a burden to her. "I shouldn't have had kids," she moaned to us as we listened, crushed. "Kids ruin your fun as well as your figure. What I could have been without kids! I was beautiful! Men were crazy for me!"

Her merciless words reverberated in my mind thereafter. They do so to this day. They seemed to me proof of what I already suspected and feared: she considered me worthless.

The fact is that, to this day, I can't really explain how my parents became what they were. But there is no denying that they were monstrously selfish. Narcissistic moral morons. No wonder I created my imaginary Toby Myers! I still wonder if I actually created Toby or based him on someone. I can't remember now. It doesn't really matter I suppose.

At last, when I was eleven and Michael nine, the domestic war took on a new pattern. Michael and I went to live with my parents in my grandfather's house in Richmond Hill in Queens. Apparently my grandfather, who had suffered a partially disabling stroke, had reluctantly agreed to allow my mother and father to share his house. But he had insisted as a condition of their living there that Michael and I be part of the household. My parents, financially desperate as usual, had complied with the sick old man's demand. No longer were Michael and I boarded out. Instead, for the first time, we saw our mysterious tormentors up close for an extended period. For the first time we observed their constant battles, verbal and physical, witnessed their dance of destruction, drinking, separation, and reconciliation. In fact we became direct participants in their vicious game. We were urged to take sides in their battles, to sympathize with one or the other. We were made participants in their struggle, made to listen to the grievances of one against the other, made to sit in judgment on their disputes, and made to hear them accuse each other of infidelity, drunkenness, theft, and a thousand acts of cruelty from their past. "Do you know she has syphilis?" my father exploded to my frozen brother and me one Sunday afternoon during a weeklong battle. "Do you know how filthy she is?" This left my brother and me heartsick.

Time after time my parents' horrid dance led to eruptions of violence in words and deeds. He would threaten her. She would jeer him. "You're a weakling. You talk big and act small." He would hit her. Michael and I would stand by helplessly, watching and crying. More often than not during these eruptions, which would sometimes last for days, my father would end matters by storming from my grandfather's house in a self-righteous fury. Often he would take me along with him to live in a hotel room for a week or two as a kind of confused and frightened hostage. In time I would be returned either upon reconciliation or further escalation of the game, i.e., upon my father's going off on a bender.

During one of these excursions, when I was a sweet-faced twelve-year-old, he left me alone in a Times Square movie house while he went out drinking. It was a seedy theater called the Laff-Movie. The place played old comedies—Laurel and Hardy, the Keystone Kops, Buster Keaton, Harold Lloyd—around the clock, seven days a week. Obedient to my father's command, I sat in the dark, alone, in the almost-deserted theater, hour after hour, waiting for him to return as promised. I didn't dare leave. I didn't know whether it was dark or light outside the Laff-Movie. I didn't know where I was. I had no money. I waited for him to come back. He didn't. A man came and sat beside me. Whispering and muttering, the man began to fondle me. I let him do as he liked. I stared at the screen, at Harold Lloyd, and tried to pretend that what was happening wasn't happening. I have forgotten the details of the event. My sister, Beth, would say that I have repressed them. I do remember, however, that Toby Myers had something to do with the experience and that it was one of the last times he played a part in my life—until the dream earlier tonight. I do remember that after (during?) the episode, I felt helpless and defiled. I hated my father. What was happening to me was his fault. I don't remember how the episode ended.

My father eventually returned, loquacious with booze, and took me to a hotel called the Dixie. I was too ashamed to tell him about the man who had touched me. I wasn't sure who I hated more, that man or my father.

At this point Gabriel lifted the pen from the paper. It had occurred to him that in writing these notes, he was not reinterring the dead after all. He was, in fact, plunging himself into the cave where they had once lain inert, and where they were now stirring to renewed life. And yet, as if the ghosts were willing it, he felt compelled to continue despite his fear of what he might be loosing. He continued to write:

I never did understand what terrible thing my mother and father wanted from each other. But I knew what Michael and I wanted: a tranquil time when we could feel loved and cared for. It never happened. My austere, widower grandfather, who despised my father as a faker and a philanderer, in which judgment he was eminently on target, tried to fill the parental gap. He would play chess with Michael and me and give us money for movies. But he was old and worn, and he was as confused as we were as to why my hate-filled parents clung to each other as they did.

Oddly, or perhaps not so oddly, despite the turmoil in our household, my sister, Beth, was born during this period. A new baby. A new hostage. When I was thirteen, my grandfather died. My parents sold his house and bought a smaller, much more modern house in New Jersey. In spite of all past experience, I found myself hoping that in our new house we would all find happiness, or at least some little peace. It didn't happen of course.

The same old pattern not only continued, but it got worse—more frequent drunken fights, more separations, more vicious threats and cruelties—and now physical violence intensified too. Now their horrible dances only ended when her goading resulted in an explosion of fists and kicks, in threats from both to kill the other. More than once Michael and I watched in petrified horror as he beat her to the floor.

As I grew older and was unable to endure my own helplessness, I began to fling myself into the middle of the flying fists and screaming threats. For some reason this was always enough to bring my father to his senses. I still carry a picture in my mind of his gaping at me as I pushed him away, the spittle gleaming on his trembling lips—and then his storming off as my mother lay on the floor bloody but still shouting her hatred at his retreating back. Strangely, despite the brutal uproar that surrounded us, Michael and I were never targets of physical abuse. Belittling words, mockery, and neglect—these were the weapons used on us. How many times did my father deride my ambition to become a writer? "What do you think you are, some kind of Hemingway? You better get your head on straight, kid. You're just daydreaming." When I won an essay contest on the subject of modern art, my mother said the work was "too silly" to read. Both were indifferent to my academic achievements at Fordham Prep, where my father had sent me in order to preen about providing a private school education for his son. The fact was that he consistently defaulted on tuition. Michael meanwhile attended the local public high school.

Finally, when I was seventeen and a senior at Fordham Prep, my mother and father, more out of exhaustion than anything else, ended their open warfare. They separated physically and permanently. Even then, however, the hateful fighting went on. But at least it now took place at a distance, through attorneys, over the phone, by mail. Now Beth became the pawn in their game, the object of a custody fight. By then I had rendered my verdict on my parents: they were beasts of selfishness. I had also resolved to escape them, to somehow inter the bitterness of my childhood.

When I graduated from Fordham Prep, I fled to Manhattan to live on my own. I worked as a copy boy at the *Daily News*. I enrolled at NYU. I dreamed of becoming a writer. In time I met Thea and began a new life with her.

Why is all this still so alive in my mind, even after forty years? Damn all this. Isn't anyone ever free?

Here Gabriel stopped. He threw the pen down on the desk lest he go on till exhaustion halted him. By this time he harbored not even a sliver of doubt that, far from reburying the dead, the words that now filled a dozen pages of his notebook had only conferred new life on the shades that dwelt in his mind. How could he have imagined it might prove otherwise? Shaken by the persistence of the past, he vowed that he would write no more, even if his ghosts howled in protest. To mark the finality of his decision, he tossed the notebook onto the couch across the room.

By now dawn had begun to show through the study window. Thea would soon be awake. Unsettled by his night's labor, Gabriel pulled a sweater over his T-shirt, slipped into a pair of running shoes, and went out into the cool air. He took some calming breaths, and then he made his way to the stream bank by the waterfall. Would he again experience the phenomenon of audible words in the torrent?

Morning light was already penetrating the woods, prompting the birds to song and spilling onto the plume of white water. Though the cataract sounded as loud and repetitive as before, it offered up no tantalizing words this time—only an innocent splashing against the rocks.

All at once a thup-thup-thup overhead drowned out both the roar of the falls and Gabriel's own thoughts. He looked up to see a DEA helicopter skimming above the hemlocks. The drug police were out early, scouring the countryside for marijuana plantings—and in the process mutilating the music of the morning. Enraged at the chopper's invasion, Gabriel turned back to the house.

CHAPTER 4

A WEEK AFTER HEARING ABOUT his brother's illness, Gabriel was in the study preparing to call Michael as promised when the phone rang. It was Yvonne.

"I phoned because I think you ought to know that, despite what Mikey hopes, he won't last six months. The doctors say he can go within a month, even sooner. I think it's only right to tell you." In a voice that seemed to have grown even raspier in the past week, she went on to detail Michael's deterioration: His feet and legs were so swollen he could no longer walk. He was in a wheelchair. Unable to take nourishment, he was becoming skeletal.

Gabriel felt his throat close up with sorrow at the picture that formed in his mind: Michael twisting and suffering in his chair. He managed to say, "Does Michael realize how bad it is?"

Yvonne said, "He knows he won't have another Christmas."

Since his dream of the Woodstock road and his failure to rebury his childhood shit under a heap of words, Gabriel had concluded that it was no use trying to guard against feeling the past when speaking on the phone to Michael. Instead he had decided to embrace his memories after all, to tell Michael that he too had been thinking about their childhood, that he'd dreamed of both of them on that road in Woodstock. Thus Gabriel had been looking forward to his scheduled conversation with his brother that day. But was Michael still able to talk? Gabriel put the question to Yvonne.

"He can still speak after he's had his shot. I know he's been looking forward to your call. But now's not a good time. Can you call later? Tonight?"

"Sure." He remembered that Michael and everyone near her called her Vonnie. Hoping she wouldn't resent his use of the name, Gabriel said, "How are you holding up, Vonnie?"

"I'm okay. Tired."

Moments later they hung up. Staring out the window, Gabriel tried to absorb the import of what he'd just heard. Michael would soon be dead. Time would end for him. He would be gone from this earth. Gabriel found it impossible to imagine the boy whose hand he'd held as their parents drove away in a Nash Rambler as a man who would soon exist no more except as a memory—or a figure in a nightmare. How could his mind grasp that?

He was alone in the house. Thea was paying a visit to Ilse and Andrus, who lived down the road. This remarkable couple, in their late eighties, had met in a refugee camp in Latvia at the end of World War II and fallen in love. Then a bureaucratic snafu had separated them. Ilse had migrated to the United States; Andrus had ended up in Australia. There he had worked for nine years as a laborer, all the time trying, through a variety of agencies, to trace his lost Ilse. Finally, in 1954, when Andrus was forty-one and Ilse thirty-nine, they had located each other. By then Ilse was an American citizen and employed as a nurse. Using her savings she traveled to Sydney, married Andrus, and brought him back with her to America. Sometime around 1970 they had purchased ten acres in Margaretville. Over the next decade they had built a log home with their own hands. They had cleared land where they grew their own food. Now nearing ninety, they were both still full of spirit and hard-won wisdom. Ilse, a tiny creature with a cap of white hair that crowned a face as furrowed as a cornfield, was always baking, planting, and weeding her garden. Andrus, short and squat, had a long face with a beaky nose and close-cropped gray hair. He spoke little, but when he did, his words were usually wise. One of his sayings had lodged in Gabriel's mind: We learn something new every day, but we still die stupid.

Thea found Ilse and Andrus fascinating, the vigor of their old age reassuring. Ilse and Andrus loved Thea in return. Ilse would grasp Thea's hand and say, "You are my golden girl. You are my warm breeze."

Gabriel considered walking down the road to join Thea at Ilse and Andrus's place. But he decided he needed to be alone to contemplate the turn of events in Missouri. In fact he wanted to drive.

He went down to the garage and backed out the Jeep. He was soon on Route 28, on the way to Margaretville. He slipped a tape into the deck, a group from the seventies, one of Thea's favorites, ABBA.

There was something in the air that night, the stars were bright, Fernando.

All at once he felt himself surging with grief for Michael's suffering and his own neglect of his brother. Then, as the music filled the car, the grief expanded into a sadness for all mortals whose lives, like his own, were no more than a piss in the ocean.

We were young and full of life, Fernando.

Tears began to flow down Gabriel's cheeks.

There was something in the air that night, Fernando.

He thought, *Michael is going to die.*

As he drove along curving Route 28, it came to him that it was one thing to write of past hurt in a notebook; it was another to feel all that pain again, as he was doing now.

The stars were bright, Fernando.

Sobbing, Gabriel thought of Andrus's saying: We learn something new every day, but we still die stupid.

Suddenly, in his head Gabriel heard a familiar voice from long ago: *We still die, Stupid.*

Toby Myers.

No doubt about it.

Resurrected in grief.

Sitting at his desk in the study that afternoon, Gabriel broke another pledge, the one to write no more of the past. It had proven a futile vow. The notebook he'd used a week earlier was still lying on the couch where he'd thrown it. He picked it up, opened it to the first of its unused pages, and printed in capital letters at the top: GABRIEL FALLON'S JOURNAL. He promised himself that no matter what he wrote on the sheets that followed, he would never revise his words. Only thus could he ensure an authentic record of what he was feeling and thinking these days. His first draft would be his only draft, the plain truth as he saw it at the moment of writing. He launched into his first entry:

I'm participating in my brother's departure from the world—in dreams, in random thoughts, in flashes of memory. This process is not only resurrecting the ghosts of my boyhood, it's also tearing away the mask behind which I've lived my life. I see now how mutilated I am. I see now why I devised a false image of myself as a writer capable of achieving great things: it was a way to compensate for the feelings of worthlessness implanted in me as a boy.

He paused. This was how his sister, Beth, with her penchant for psych-speak would explain his history. Still, what he had just written was true. His belief in himself as a writer had been a false front he'd erected to give himself significance. He returned to the journal.

If I'd not deluded myself all these years about being a serious writer, would life have been worth living? Would I have found Thea? No. But now the fantasy is smashed to bits, thanks to the fiasco of *Avernus*. And Michael's dying, by opening the closed gates of the past, has allowed me to discover that all my falseness grew from the wounds of a young boy. Is it time to put to rest the boy I once was? How? Suicide? There, I've written the word. Suicide. Write it again. Suicide. Is this the way to relieve the self of the self? If so, why am I so afraid of it, even as it tempts me? And am I willing to inflict pain on Thea and on my children to relieve myself?

I would like to put these questions to God—if I believed in God. The truth is that I want to believe in God but can't. Why? Is it because my heart is too hard? Why can't I simply speak to God as other people seem to do? Why can't I say, "Here I am God? If you want me, I'm here." Is it possible that God also considers me worthless? Or is God not here for me just because I can't bring myself to believe in him as other people do? Circular reasoning: God's not here for me because I don't believe in him; I don't believe in him because he's not here for me.

I have to caution myself—be honest in these pages. Keep these jottings true, no matter how wildly they may veer about in my disturbed psyche. Otherwise, of what value are these notes? I mustn't be a faker like my father. Truth now. Cold and simple. And no whining either!

Gabriel stopped. He could write no more—for a while. He closed the notebook and put it away in a drawer of his desk.

That night Gabriel called his brother in Missouri, making the call from the kitchen while Thea, a flowered apron over her jeans, went about baking cookies in anticipation of the arrival of the grandchildren in a few days. When he came on the phone, Michael sounded worn but lucid.

"Hi, Gabe, I guess you heard I'm not going to make it till Christmas."

"I heard."

"Strange, Gabe, I keep thinking about Woodstock. Funky town. Despite everything bad that happened to us there, it was a good place to grow up. Odd that you live so close to the old place now. You must have driven over to take a gander. How does it look these days?"

In fact Thea and Gabriel had visited Woodstock only once during their stay in the Catskills. The town had changed greatly from the village that Michael and Gabriel had known. It was now a theme park for New Agers. Only the patch of village green with its white-painted church seemed untouched. When Gabriel told this to his brother, Michael sighed and said, "Well, for me the town is still what it was forty years ago."

The brothers began to reminisce about the Woodstock they had known, focusing on the months they spent with a certain Mrs. Keller, a stout, good-natured (for the most part) woman who supplemented her farm income by boarding troubled children for the county. This was how young Gabe had heard Mrs. Keller describe her function back then. Later he had discovered from eavesdropping on Mrs. Keller's complaints that his parents had persuaded the Kellers to take in young Gabe and Michael, even though the boys were neither troubled (officially) nor under the jurisdiction of the dreaded county.

Originally Michael and Gabriel were to remain at the Keller farm for only six weeks, but their stay had lengthened to almost a year until their parents' delinquency on board payments resulted in the removal of the boys.

Mrs. Keller, whose household consisted of herself, her taciturn Indian husband, Ollie, and her fourteen-year-old son Jake, dealt simply with all her young charges: she fed their bodies with wholesome food and their spirits with Calvinist admonitions. Mrs. Keller also kept an aged brassbound telescope—a spyglass she called it—mounted in her parlor. With this instrument trained on the town of Woodstock sprawled below her mountainside, she often spent hours at a time snooping on her neighbors.

When Gabriel reminded Michael of this, he laughed. "Oh, God. The telescope! What a busybody she was, our God-fearing Mrs. Keller! Despite it all, Gabe, we did have fun!"

Gabriel listened with a grief-stopped throat as Michael now burbled on about ice skating on frozen ponds, swimming in a water-filled stone quarry, and crossing a river on a tremulous log bridge with young Jake Keller, whom both he and young Gabe had hero-worshipped. Michael even recalled an afternoon when, to the brothers' delight, heroic Jake had used his Boy Scout knife to decapitate a copperhead that was sunning itself on a rock.

Suddenly Michael said, "Do you remember Hazel?"

Gabriel pictured a pretty blonde girl in her teens who had been a county ward at the Keller establishment while they had resided there. Very pale with precociously shapely breasts and body, Hazel was the first girl who'd ever inspired sexual thoughts in Gabriel. Her light blonde hair had been cut so short that it resembled a furry cap. She always seemed to be dressed in flowery dresses that were too big for her—probably because they were castoffs from a variety of charities. Except in winter, when the county provided shoes, Hazel went about with bare feet. She was shy with adults, but when alone with Jake Keller, she became a giggling tease. She encouraged Jake to kiss her and touch her in places that even young Gabe, at eight years old, recognized as forbidden.

Jake had sworn young Gabe to secrecy about his feeling up Hazel. True to his oath, young Gabe had never breathed a word about it to any adult. In return for his silence, Jake had permitted young Gabe to stand guard whenever he and Hazel were making out in the hayloft or elsewhere. Young Gabe thoroughly enjoyed his role as lookout—for not only could he serve Jake in this way, he could also look upon Hazel, relishing the sexual warmth stirred in him by the sight of her pale legs exposed by her hiked-up dress. Often as he stood guard, young Gabe sensed that Hazel enjoyed his eyes on her—for she would smile at him and arrange herself to make sure that he also saw everything she was showing to Jake. Often Toby Myers would also appear during these sessions. Young Gabe and Toby would whisper together about Hazel's pretty legs and "peachy tits," Toby's phrase.

Suddenly there rose from Gabriel's memory a picture of Toby caressing Hazel's breast with his paralyzed hand, and her simpering impudently as young Gabe looked on red-faced. Of course Gabriel told himself now that nothing like that had ever really happened. Toby was imaginary, even if poor Hazel wasn't. Anything he remembered about Toby engaged in sexual play with Hazel had to be only a recollection of young Gabe's own fantasies about her. Toby had never really touched Hazel any more than young Gabe had. They had only watched Hazel and Jake together. But a shred of doubt lingered. What if young Gabe had touched Hazel and then attributed the misdemeanor to his invented companion? Disturbing as he found it, Gabriel realized he could not be absolutely sure of young Gabe's innocence back then.

But of Hazel's precociousness, he was certain. Unlike other wards of the county who passed quickly through the Keller household, Hazel stayed on, a special case. Later, looking back as an adult, Gabriel had surmised that some child abuser had induced Hazel's premature sexuality and it was to protect her from the consequences of her own behavior that the county had placed her with Mrs. Keller.

Hazel? Of course Gabriel remembered Hazel.

Michael said, "What do you think ever happened to Hazel?"

Gabriel said, "I hope she got married and lived happily ever after." But in fact he suspected that Hazel's destiny had been less happy. The Hazels of the world seldom managed to heal their early wounds.

Michael said, "I like to think she grew up to be a movie star. Yeah. She dyed her hair and changed her name for the screen and we just never recognized her in the movies." He laughed at his own suggestion. The laugh triggered in Gabriel's mind an image of his brother as he'd been when young Gabe and Toby had spied on Hazel and Jake Keller: short and chunky, thick brown hair, and—unlike most other Fallon males—freckled. With this picture of Michael in his mind's eye, and hearing his voice still strong, his speech lucid, Gabriel found it hard to envision his brother as the skeletal figure that Yvonne had described. And yet, that was the reality, not the boy from Woodstock.

With another laugh, Michael said, "I'm sure our buddy Jake did okay."

"Jake Keller? He probably joined the marines."

"Yeah, semper fi. I can just picture him with the special forces in Vietnam." He was silent for a moment, and then said, "Yeah, it was a good place, Woodstock. I wish I could see it again."

The note of sadness in Michael's voice was the first expression of sorrow Gabriel had detected in him. What prompted it? Fear? Regret for the flow of time? As much as he would have liked to ask, Gabriel held his tongue. Let Michael decide if he wanted to talk of such matters. It was his death they were preparing. But Michael seemed to have no more to say.

To break the silence—which felt like a harbinger of the eternity to come—Gabriel asked if Michael remembered a boy named Toby Myers. Maybe Michael could identify the real Toby, if one ever existed, on whom Gabriel might have based his imaginary playmate.

"Toby? Myers? Nope. Don't know him."

Gabriel suggested that Toby might have been a friend of Jake Keller's or a visitor to the Keller house, even one of the transient county wards.

"Nope. Never heard of him. Why do you ask?"

"Oh, I've been having some weird dreams lately. This crippled kid, Toby Myers, has been in them. I have him pegged as an imaginary playmate of mine long ago, but sometimes I wonder if my memory's playing tricks about that. Maybe he was a real kid after all, or where did I get that name Toby Myers?"

"Damned if I know, Gabe. You were always inventing stories, pretending to see ghosts. Maybe he's from one of your ghost stories." He laughed. "You could be a pretty scary kid back then, Gabe. You used to scare me anyway."

Toby Myers a ghost? A ghost of Gabriel's childhood certainly but a mystery otherwise.

In response to a question, Gabriel told his brother that Richard, Joyce, and the grandchildren, as well as Valerie, would be visiting him and Thea over the Fourth of July holiday.

Michael said, "I hear your son makes a lot of money."

"Yes." Gabriel didn't tell him that Richard and his wife had become fundamentalist Christians and moved with their children to a run-down Chicago neighborhood in order to spend their money doing God's work, which had entailed establishment of a storefront church.

Michael said, "Money's nice but family's what counts."

A question that Gabriel hadn't intended to ask burst out of him. "Michael, do you believe in God?"

"That's another question people keep asking me now. Sometimes I believe and sometimes I don't. But I'm trying harder than ever to believe. How 'bout you?"

Thinking of his journal entry, Gabriel said, "I want to believe. I wish God would show his face. I wish I knew how to reach him."

"You're a writer. Write to him. Might work." This remark was followed by a sigh and Gabriel realized that his brother was tired. Or perhaps it was time for his medication. Gabriel promised to call again in a few days. They hung up.

During Gabriel's talk with Michael, Thea had continued with baking her cookies while listening. She now came over and gave Gabriel a hug as he sat on the stool. She said, "You're discovering you can't bury the childhood shit, Gabe, try as you will. I still cry when I think of the years I spent in foster homes. Sometimes I think human beings are like trees. If we're lucky we grow. We dig down roots. We thicken with the years, growth ring upon growth ring, but our original form, those early rings, they're in us forever."

CHAPTER 5

THE NEXT MORNING WHILE in his study, it came to Gabriel that he might make a bargain with God about believing in him. Of course he knew that the drill in such matters, the Faustian method, called for making a deal with the devil. But Gabriel was sure that, despite the world's evil, the devil did not exist; he was merely an excuse for the malignity of humankind.

The existence of God, however, was an open question, for it seemed at least plausible that the universe might have required a creator to set in motion the big bang. Thus, why not give God a try? What did he have to lose? True, Gabriel had always considered the universe and its creator, if there was one, essentially unknowable. But what if he was wrong about that? What if God was only waiting for him to reach out before showing himself? Maybe God liked a challenge, liked doing business with nonbelievers.

With these none-too-coherent thoughts in mind, Gabriel murmured a proposition to the empty room: "Help me to become a serious writer, God. Grant me *that* salvation and I'll believe in you." Having uttered this proposal—prayer?—he thought, *Okay, God, You'll probably turn out to be an impostor, but it's up to you now. Do your stuff.*

It was a joke, but not a joke.

Young Gabe is nine years old. He is in bed at the Keller house. It is a winter night. There is ice on the single window in the bedroom that he shares with his brother, Michael, who sleeps rolled up in blankets in his cot across the room. Young Gabe is lying on his back in his own cot. He is staring into the dark. Tense and frightened, he is listening to voices in the parlor below. The voices reach him through the heat grate in the bedroom floor.

"What we goin' to do about them boys?" This is Mrs. Keller. Young Gabe pictures her sitting in her easy chair near the stove. She is wearing her red woolen shawl. She is knitting. It is what she likes to do on winter evenings. Ollie is there with her, as he always is. He is smoking his pipe. He is wearing clean overalls for the parlor.

Suddenly Toby Myers joins young Gabe in the bed. *What's up, pal?*

As if in answer to Toby, Mrs. Keller's voice rises again through the grate. "Been four months now since we got some board money from the ma and pa."

"You telephone them?" This is Ollie's voice, softer than his wife's.

"Of course I telephoned them. And wrote too. They ain't to be found."

"So?"

"So we can't afford to feed those boys, clothe 'em, give 'em shelter."

"Bible says we ought to though, don't it?"

"Bible says no such thing. The mother and father supposed to do that."

"So?"

"So we can't keep those boys here forever. It ain't right."

"I guess it ain't."

"The county'll have to take 'em."

At these words young Gabe's heart jumps in his chest like a startled rabbit. He covers his ears with his hands to shut out the voices from below. He doesn't dare listen to more. The county—he is terrified of the county. Hazel has told him that when the county had her they whipped her and did other things too terrible to explain. Now the county is to have him and Michael. Tears leap into Young Gabe's eyes.

Toby says, *If you didn't have to watch over Michael, we could run away.*

Young Gabe looks over at Michael asleep in the other cot.

Toby says, *Jake would help us run away. Jake knows all the good places where we could hide.*

All at once young Gabe feels anger because his brother can't run, can't hide, can't do anything. Then he remembers her saying, "Take care of Michael." He is ashamed. All right, he will take care of Michael. But where is *she* now? Why is she letting Mrs. Keller send Michael and him to the county?

Toby says, *Your stomach is starting to ache, right? I can tell.*

Young Gabe whispers to Toby, "Why doesn't anyone want Michael and me?"

Because you're stupid, Stupid. Toby giggles at his own joke.

Closing his eyes, young Gabe wishes hard to escape, to be somewhere else, somewhere safe.

In response Toby gets out of the bed. He takes young Gabe's hand in his good left hand. *Come on, pal, let's get out of here.*

Young Gabe feels himself wafting up from the bed, out from under the covers. He is floating in the air as if swimming in nothingness. Wearing only his underpants and T-shirt—his customary bedclothes—he and Toby glide to the window. Flowers of frost cover the pane, rendering it opaque. He and Toby hover before it for a moment and then swim through the glass into the night. Below them, silent fields white with snow drift by. Then, willing himself to go, go, go, young Gabe picks up speed until, shivering, he is flying across the world like Captain Marvel. Toby flying with him shouts, *Shazam!* They are rushing through the night, away from the Kellers, away from Michael. They are escaping. Inflated with joy, young Gabe doesn't feel the wind that freezes his skin. He will soar through the stars and never stop. He will fly forever across the snowfields. Shazam!

But then young Gabe pulls up, his skinny boy's body hanging in midair.

Toby says, *You got no place to go, Stupid!* He laughs and says, *Boy, you are dumb, pal!*

At once young Gabe realizes he has no destination. There is no one who wants him except Michael. And so, bones rattling with cold, he drifts back through the glass into the bedroom where Michael still sleeps.

He is once more beneath the covers of his cot with Toby who says, *Boy, you are dumb, Stupid!*

Young Gabe has learned that even if he can fly across the world, he has no place to go. Shazam.

Gabriel came to himself again in Margaretville in bed with Thea. The clock across the room read 3:28 a.m. His stomach was aching as it had that night more than forty years earlier when he'd heard Mrs. Keller talking to Ollie about sending Michael and him to the county shelter. He felt his heart flopping under his ribs. Another memory dream. Another experience relived with Toby. Yes, Toby was present that night as he had been most of the time back then. No doubt of it now: the ghosts were at large.

Gabriel couldn't stay in bed any longer. Careful not to disturb Thea, he slipped out from under the covers. To his surprise he had no desire for booze despite the disquiet in his gut. He put on a robe and slippers. He went downstairs and then out into the night.

A slice of moon cruised among the clouds. Gabriel could hear Eternity Falls pounding upstream. Trying to slow his heart, he breathed deeply—but the thumping worsened. He felt a thrill of fear. Was he about to confound the doctors and die of his arrhythmia? After so much pondering of suicide, why did he still shrink from the dissolution of his body?

He thought, *Be calm, be calm. It's just a worsening of the fibrillation brought on by stress, by memories and dreams. Breathe. Breathe and be calm. Think of something else. Think about Toby.* Why had Toby invaded his dreams? But thinking of Toby wasn't going to help him. Fuck Toby. Fucking figment.

Gabriel made his way to the falls. Dew soaked his slippers as he walked. Something scurried away before him. He stood by the cataract, its white plume just visible in the weak moonlight. He listened to its rhythm, the same notes repeating themselves. Suddenly he again detected what sounded like words in the thunder before him. It seemed to be the same phrase that he had perceived previously—an incantation emanating from the boom but just beneath the horizon of comprehension, as if the waterfall was trying to communicate. He found it mesmerizing. Of course reason could explain it readily enough: the waterfall wasn't actually producing words but only hitting the rocks in such a way as to create a pattern of noises that struck his ear like a sequence of syllables. A rational interpretation, he told himself, but not necessarily the true one.

By degrees the phenomenon faded away as the torrent resumed an unequivocal roaring. Gabriel's heart also slowed, and he thought, *It was only an illusion. Only an effect of stress. Like my dreams. Like Toby.*

A breeze came up, sighing through the woods. Gabriel went back to the house.

CHAPTER 6

O N THE AFTERNOON OF July third Thea and Gabriel drove to Margaretville to rendezvous with Richard, Joyce, and the grandchildren. The plan was to have lunch with them, and then take them to the house that all of them would be sharing for the next week.

As worked out by Thea and Joyce, the Midwest Fallons (as Joyce called her brood) were flying directly from Chicago to the small airfield that served much of the Catskills, Stewart Airport in Newburgh. They would then drive a rental car to Margaretville where Thea and Gabriel were to meet them around 2:00 p.m. at a restaurant called the Inn. Thea had chosen this place because it stood just off Route 28 and Richard could find it easily—and also because it served hamburgers and other grease-laden foods that the grandchildren relished.

While Gabriel wore jeans, a long-sleeved shirt, and running shoes, Thea had prepared herself with care for the occasion. She had arranged her hair in a ponytail and adorned her face with lipstick and eyeliner. In addition she had dressed herself elegantly in a pleated, white linen skirt, a sleeveless white blouse, and a pair of white sandals.

Gabriel parked the Jeep in the lot of the Inn. He said to her, "You sure don't look like any grandma I know." Thea beamed as the two of them exited the Jeep to await the Midwest Fallons.

Minutes later Richard drove up in a white Taurus. The kids, Benji and Miriam, tumbled out of the car. Squealing with laughter, dressed in shorts, sneakers, and identical blue T-shirts that bore the words "We love Grandma," they ran to embrace Thea, who knelt to squeeze them to her. They then embraced Gabriel as well. Six-year-old Benji, fair-haired, brown-eyed, small for his age and a bundle of exuberance, jumped into Gabriel's arms and wrapped his legs around his waist. Miriam, a pixie-faced, knobby-kneed eight-year-old with blue eyes peeping from under blonde bangs, bestowed a kiss on Gabriel's cheek. He noted, not for the first time, that despite their family name neither of the children resembled their Fallon forebears. With his brown eyes and small frame, Benji looked like his mother, while Miriam favored Thea more than anyone else.

Joyce, in jeans and plaid shirt, and Richard, looking tired in slacks and a beige windbreaker, took turns hugging Thea and Gabriel. Then the six of them went into the Inn to have lunch before going on to the house. The children could barely contain themselves as they ate hamburgers; they were so excited about seeing Grandma and Grandpa's house that stood in the woods—and had a waterfall!

As lunch proceeded, the kids chattering about school and friends and pets, Gabriel took the opportunity to gaze around the table at this family of his.

Benji, whom he hadn't seen in six months, not since Christmas in Chicago, seemed somewhat better behaved than he'd been at Christmas but still willful and loud. Miriam had grown taller. Her smile was as sweet as ever, her intelligence still veiled under a serene but oh-so-watchful exterior. It seemed to Gabriel that Miriam was one of those who was always listening, always aware—even when they appeared withdrawn. He had to admit that Miriam was his favorite, not only because of her resemblance to Thea but even more because he sensed Thea's lovable acuity budding in her.

Richard, approaching his mid-thirties now, not as tall as his father and with a shock of brown hair, seemed to have aged somewhat since Gabriel had seen him last. He had also acquired a short beard that imparted an even squarer shape to his Fallonesque features. Gabriel noted that gray already dappled his son's beard, and his hazel eyes behind the horn-rimmed glasses appeared dull with fatigue. Gabriel also saw that his son was developing a paunch. Richard, he reflected, looked like the highly stressed entrepreneur that he was. However Gabriel happily noted that Richard's humor seemed undiminished, judging by his banter with Thea, Joyce, and the children. At one point in the luncheon Richard leaned to Gabriel and said, "Dad, you have my oath that during this visit I won't use my cell phone and won't even mention clients or the market."

Gabriel was glad to hear it. He was anticipating some serious conversation with Richard, during which he hoped to learn more about the interior of this son whose life for the past decade had seemed such a puzzle to him.

Twelve years earlier, Richard (already married to Joyce) had crowned a brilliant academic career by achieving acceptance to Harvard Medical School. Ever since boyhood Richard had aspired to become a doctor, envisioning himself as a healer dedicated to the alleviation of suffering. But at the start of his second year in med school, he had astounded all who knew him—and his father most of all—by casting aside his studies. A shocked Gabriel had urged him to reconsider. But Richard had refused, saying, "I'm sorry, Dad, but I just can't see myself playing God in a white coat for the rest of my life." Even Thea could not get him to say more about his decision.

Richard had then provoked further astonishment by throwing himself into the world of money. Again he had declined to set forth his reasons, except to say, "This is just something I have to do for Joyce and myself."

Applying his talents for the abstract, Richard had prospered as a trader in the stock market. And then, on the verge of opulence, his life had taken still another turn into the extraordinary.

In the wake of his wife's conversion to evangelical Christianity, Richard had become a religious enthusiast. Under pressure from Joyce, he had moved his family to Chicago for the purpose of "serving the Lord."

His sister, Valerie, had chided him at the time: "You've made yourself one of the deluded."

Richard had responded with a smile. "Not so, Val. The fact is I now have eyes to see the truth and the will to do good." But as before, he declined to elaborate.

Despite Richard's refusal to explain his journey from Cambridge to Chicago, Gabriel never doubted the authenticity of his metamorphosis. He had long ago discovered—to his relief—that his son had escaped the Fallon propensity to embellish and preen. In fact, on those occasions when Richard had revealed some aspect of himself, he had done so with a modesty alien to most Fallons. Still, Richard's reticence about his life over the past decade had made him an enigma to his father. Thus Gabriel hoped—admittedly without much cause—that during this Fourth of July visit his son would afford him an opportunity to see into his interior.

Gabriel also wanted to learn more about Joyce, a woman he had never been able to fathom. A year older than Richard, Joyce was a Texan with a degree in architecture—though she had never practiced her profession. Like Thea and Gabriel, Joyce and Richard had married young, while both were undergraduates. They had been together now for thirteen years. Joyce, who still spoke with a Texas drawl, often seemed delicate to Gabriel. Fair-skinned and freckled, she wore her reddish-brown hair short and brushed back in no-nonsense style. Though no one was likely to call Joyce pretty, despite her heart-shaped face, she possessed one striking physical attribute: eyes of a brown so pale they seemed to verge on yellow. In certain lights they reminded Gabriel of cat's eyes, luminous and remote—as if she was forever peering out to some far off vista.

In dress, Joyce favored jeans and plaid shirts. She had abandoned architecture some years earlier—as soon as Richard's income made it feasible—in order to devote herself to raising Miriam and Benji.

Even after thirteen years of contact, Gabriel still didn't know what to make of Joyce. He thought her intelligent, if not well read. But she insisted that the Bible not only represented the literal word of God, but it was the only guide permitted for navigating life. Apparently she had converted Richard to her point of view by hammering at his skepticism until he collapsed into acquiescence, a turn of events that left Gabriel dumbfounded. How could his son, so well-educated, well-traveled, and sophisticated, embrace such absurdities as God's halting the sun so Joshua could finish off the defenders of Jericho? But clearly Richard did embrace it, for if asked about such nonsense, he would only smile and say, "God can do anything." Obviously Joyce had won the battle for his soul. Nor had she stopped there.

Two years ago, after what she called a vision from God, Joyce had demanded that the Midwest Fallons move from their suburban home to Chicago's Bucktown section—a black and Hispanic neighborhood considered one of the city's most crime-ridden, despite a recent spate of gentrification. Richard and Joyce had bought and renovated a dilapidated townhouse in Bucktown. They had enrolled the children in a private Christian school in a better neighborhood. Then, again at Joyce's instigation, they had set about establishing a church-cum-shelter for the homeless and battered that they named Holy Harbor Congregation. This church-shelter had since closed under circumstances that neither Joyce nor Richard would discuss, but Gabriel hoped they would tell the story during their Fourth of July visit.

Though Joyce often stunned Gabriel with the fervor of her fundamentalism, nothing had astonished him more than her revelation made during that Christmas visit to Chicago last year. She claimed that she routinely observed, with what she termed her spiritual eyes, immaterial entities hovering around her and her children. These beings, she informed Gabriel, made their way about the globe, indeed about the universe, in the service of God (angels, Gabriel supposed) or in the employ of the devil (demons, no doubt).

At first Gabriel persuaded himself that she was speaking metaphorically. But then one afternoon when he and Joyce were alone in the kitchen, she told him a tale that convinced him she meant her words literally: While driving through one of Chicago's seediest areas, a voice had instructed her to pick up a vagabond (her term) hitchhiking at an intersection. Toothless, reeking of urine, and toting a bag of rags, the vagrant had seated himself beside her in the car. As she drove, he sat in silence, his stink gagging her. And then Joyce had seen glory descend on her passenger: "He shone with light and he now wore robes of snowy white. And I knew this was an angel of the Lord come to deliver a message to me." Gabriel asked what the angel had told her.

"That I was to pray hard and serve God in this terrible city of Chicago, that the Lord would guide Richard and me. Then the angel reassumed his guise as a homeless man, and I let him out of the car. I drove away filled with love for the Lord God."

After that Gabriel had come to accept that she genuinely believed she could behold with her spiritual eyes a cosmic struggle between angels and demons. Gabriel found Joyce's interior world disturbing, but he also found Joyce herself kind, generous, and a loving mother. What manner of wife she might be, Gabriel could only guess, but Richard seemed content enough. The truth was that Joyce fascinated Gabriel, and he hoped to get to know her better in the days ahead.

After lunch Gabriel drove Thea and the children to the house, while Richard and Joyce followed in the Taurus. After parking the cars in the lee of the house, Thea helped Joyce and Richard settle into their quarters while Gabriel remained outside with the children.

Miriam and Benji gazed about them, absorbing the reality of this place they had only imagined until this moment. Gabriel sensed that as they looked at the house surrounded by boulders and grim woods, all of it appeared to them huge and perhaps a little frightening—like the castle of a giant.

To break the spell, he offered to show them the falls—whose pounding they could hear behind a stand of hemlocks. When the torrent came into view before them, both children halted in awe. As if to enhance the effect of the scene, Gabriel intoned the name: "Eternity Falls." He almost added, 'Behold!'

Her eyes big with wonder, Miriam stared at the column of water. But Benji, recovering from astonishment, whooped with glee. "I want to wade in the river, Grandpa!"

Gabriel saw no reason why he shouldn't. The stream was fast flowing but afforded a number of shallows where the boy could play in safety. Gabriel sent him to ask his mother's permission to go wading. Benji ran off. Miriam continued to watch the cataract, as if entranced.

Benji reappeared in a diminutive red swimsuit. "Mom says it's okay to go in, Grandpa, if you're watching!" Without waiting for Gabriel's reply, he splashed into the water.

As Gabriel watched from the bank and Miriam observed, Benji began to make his way upstream toward the falls. Though he kept to the channels of least turbulence, he still had to fight against the current that swirled about his legs. Despite this impediment, however, Benji soon approached the parapet where the cataract began its fall. Here he halted and looked up at the wall of water crashing down only ten or twelve feet from him—as if pouring from the sky. Gabriel tried to imagine how gigantic, and thus intimidating, Eternity Falls probably looked to the child poised in the vicinity of its thunder. He smiled, assuming that for all his audacity, Benji would now retreat from the fury before him. Instead the boy struggled even closer to the cascade. Alarmed, Gabriel called down to him. "That's far enough, Benji!" But Benji, pretending he hadn't heard, toiled on.

Frightened for his grandson's safety and angry at his disobedience as well, Gabriel again shouted for him to get back. But Benji, still ignoring the warning, plopped himself into the white water where the falls smashed onto the rock slabs below—and instantly went whirling away. Gabriel's heart leaped at the sight. He was about to throw himself into the stream to rescue Benji when he realized that, far from hurt or frightened, the boy found the ride thrilling. His squeals signified glee not terror.

Coming to rest downstream, Benji jumped to his feet. "That was great, Grandpa! I'm going again!" Benji's joy in his feat dissipated both Gabriel's panic and anger. In silence he played sentinel from the bank as Benji continued to duck, slip, and slide about in the cataract's white water. After a few more minutes of watching this merry—and as it turned out quite safe—exercise, Miriam ran to the house to fetch her own bathing suit.

Soon, as Benji went on frolicking below him, Gabriel once more began to detect indistinct words in the roar of the falling water. Despite the explanation for the effect that he had given himself the night before, he couldn't help trying to make sense of the syllables the torrent seemed to carry. He employed a process that produced results when he tried to recall the lyrics of a song: get the pattern right, the tempo and rhythm in line, the melody clear, and the lyric would come back. But this time the method failed. The words in Eternity Falls, if they were there, continued to elude him. They were probably only a tantalizing illusion anyway. But what if they weren't? What if, against all reason, the falling water was generating a message? What if it was the voice of God in the falls? What if God had chosen this method to respond to Gabriel's proposition? If God existed, who could tell how he might make himself known?

It came to Gabriel that if he let himself into the stream, down into the clamor, he might improve his chances of deciphering the puzzle. He started to climb down the embankment, but just at the margin of the flow, dread seized him. He froze, incapable of taking the step that would put him into the current. Suppose once in the stream he found himself drawn into the torrent's embrace? Might the experience shock his fibrillating heart enough to kill him? But so what if it killed him? He was contemplating an end to his life anyway, wasn't he? But was he really? Honestly? Or was all that a pose? Breathing hard, he scrambled back up the bank to safety. The day might come when he'd find the courage to go down there where Benji was romping but not today—even if it was God speaking in the cataract.

Later, as the others gathered for dinner, Gabriel went to the study and wrote in his journal.

For reasons I can't fathom yet, my drinking has tapered off in the last week or so, much to Thea's relief. And I should expect that, on that account alone, my mind would begin to revert to a more or less rational clarity. But it seems that exactly the opposite is happening. Take for example the latent words I hear in the waterfall. Are they really there? Or is the stress of my life's failure making me as susceptible to illusion as Joyce is with her angels and demons? Of course common sense tells me that the idea of actual words emanating from the waterfall is an absurdity. Yet some part of me rejects reason in this matter. That part of me—which is no doubt producing my strangely intelligible dreams as well—this increasingly fanciful part of me wants the waterfall to be offering a message to me. And as crazy as it may be, I find I can't just dismiss the possibility that God might be trying to talk to me in the waterfall. I have to find out, one way or another: Is Eternity Falls calling to me, or is all this just a watery delusion? And how am I to obtain an answer to that question?

Here he lifted his pen from the paper, for the answer had suddenly bloomed in his mind. As if vouchsafed by some unknown but undeniable source, he knew beyond doubt that if he was ever to resolve the mystery of the waterfall words, he would have to do precisely what he'd been unable to do that afternoon: he had to make himself go to Eternity Falls and let it pound down on him in a ritual of bravery. Admittedly this was an irrational idea. But rationality seemed to have little to do with his state of mind these days. Had he not resurrected Toby Myers in his dreams? Didn't the blackest of thoughts swim like sharks in the pools of his mind? Yes, no matter what the danger, he simply had to go under the falling water—only there might he capture the words. Of course the waterfall ordeal might kill him, but it also might wash away his despair in a baptism of redemption. He resumed writing.

I must submit to the falls—death or redemption. But what if I find some other fate there? What if I encounter one of Joyce's devils hidden behind the curtain of water? What if a nymph's cave opens in the rocks behind the cataract and swallows me? What if the waterfall is carrying a message that turns out to be some truth I can't endure? And now, at last, a question from what remains of my rational self: what if, despite the lessening of my drinking, I'm losing my grip on reality altogether? I suppose it all comes down to this: I've got to rid myself of uncertainty. I have to go under the falls to do it. When? That I don't know. When I have the guts, I guess. In the meantime, I'll keep listening to the waterfall. Maybe God's there, ready to make a believer of me. Or maybe I'll find some way to decode the message without going under. Or maybe I'll go completely crazy and none of this will matter in the asylum.

Addressing Thea and Gabriel, Richard said, "Why don't you two come and stay with us in Chicago?"

The four adults were lingering at the dining room table after dinner on the first evening of Joyce and Richard's visit. The children, visible through the un-curtained windows, were outside chasing fireflies in the twilight.

Aware of Gabriel's reluctance to accept his long-standing invitation to live with the Midwest Fallons, Richard pressed further. "Come on, Dad, give in. You and Mom say you're finished with the Catskills, so why not give Chicago a try? You can stay in our guest apartment. Very elaborate now. The kids would love the arrangement."

Thea beamed her approval.

Though touched by his son's proposal, Gabriel was unwilling to discuss it while his mind was seething with other matters. He said, "It's all very generous, Richard. Okay if we think it over?"

As if he had expected his father's response, Richard nodded, and Gabriel changed the subject by asking once again about the demise of Holy Harbor Congregation. He had never heard the story of the failure of this storefront church-cum-shelter that Richard and Joyce had set up in their Bucktown neighborhood, though he knew much of its history.

To begin with, he knew that, under the aegis of a denomination compatible with Joyce's fundamentalism, Richard had rehabilitated a former dry cleaning store on Ashland Avenue in a district of crumbling shops, Hispanic travel agencies, and check-cashing establishments. He also knew that, with Richard paying all expenses, including the salary of a minister known as Pastor Tom, Holy Harbor church-shelter had soon attracted some thirty communicants—all of them indigents from the neighborhood.

Gabriel had had the opportunity to form his own impressions of the enterprise last Christmas when he and Thea had attended several services with Richard, Joyce, and the children. Gabriel had enjoyed the clapping and singing—and even the lectern-pounding sermons by Pastor Tom. Holy Harbor, battling drugs, violence, and poverty, had seemed to be thriving then.

But it hadn't lasted. Somehow Holy Harbor had gone wrong. Richard and Joyce had withdrawn from the church-and-shelter they had founded. They had never revealed why. And even now, seated at the table after dinner in Margaretville, their reluctance to tell the story continued.

In response to Gabriel's query, Richard only said, "Joyce and I are okay with what happened at Holy Harbor, Dad. It's what God wanted. I'm sure of that. Just as I'm sure God means us to stay in Bucktown."

Thea said, "Enough serious talk. Let's go out and help the kids catch fireflies."

That night in bed Thea pressed Gabriel about Chicago. "Why don't we just go out there and explore the city for a while? Then we can look for our own place. Maybe we'll find a real paradise." Gabriel told her he had other matters on his mind. She put her hand in his. "Michael."

He felt a sudden urge to tell her about the words in the falls and that he had made up his mind to immerse himself in the torrent to decipher them. But Thea, he knew, would declare against it. She would call it a stupid stunt, and she would warn him of the shock the cataract might deliver to his heart. In the end she'd probably convince him to call it off. He already had enough misgivings about the waterfall baptism without Thea's adding more. He decided to say nothing to her yet about any of it.

Thea said, "Oh, I forgot to tell you. Valerie phoned. She's going to arrive the day after tomorrow."

Gabriel pictured this daughter whom he adored but often found difficult. Valerie was not a beauty like her mother but an attractive amalgam of parental genes; and thus her face, oval-shaped like her mother's, also reprised the squarish chin, broad brow, and straight nose of the Fallon clan. But her eyes were all Thea's: a vivid blue. Her brown hair, a mix of her mother's honey and the wine-dark of most Fallons, swirled about a countenance too often glum these days. Taller than her mother, Val was ample-breasted, flat-bellied, and long-legged. She moved with the ease of an athlete. She had always been a girl who would rather play the game than lead cheers. She was also a girl who both charmed and intimidated most males.

As with Richard, Valerie had not chosen the life Gabriel would have predicted for her. As a student, she had plowed through schoolwork without strain. She'd also been pretty (still was) popular and talented in a variety of ways. Gabriel had expected her to make a career in the theater, writing plays or acting. But she had surprised him by opting for a life in the science of zoology. Overnight, or so it had seemed, she had gone from accomplished golden girl to thin-skinned feminist. Gabriel often thought that, for some reason unknown to him, Val had forced herself to become a scientist. It seemed to him that by nature she was too impatient, too imaginative, and too mercurial to derive satisfaction from the plodding of science. But he had accepted her redefinition of herself because he loved her, whatever she made of her life.

Over the last few years, while in pursuit of advanced degrees at Columbia, Val had launched herself into a skein of love affairs. Each had crashed and burned for reasons that she pronounced incomprehensible but which Gabriel attributed to her poor choice of lovers. Saying that too much love gone wrong (her phrase) had soured her, Val now lived what she called a monastic life in the city. Lonely and broke but rejecting help from her parents, she spent her days scrambling after her doctorate. Gabriel clung to the hope that one day she would allow her golden-girl persona to emerge again so that, restored to her natural brightness, she could escape the misery of her current existence. For the sake of this hope he made it a practice to endure Val's moods and often-erratic behavior. He looked forward to her visit, convinced that it would do her good to play Auntie Val for a few days with Miriam and Benji. He started to say as much to Thea but she had already fallen asleep.

CHAPTER 7

THE FOURTH OF JULY was a sticky, grayish day that carried a threat of late thunderstorms. Gabriel spent the morning lazing about the living room with Richard and Joyce, both of whom were reading—Richard a history of computers, Joyce a religious tract on the nature of angels.

As the morning dragged on, Gabriel stared out a window at the gathering clouds. From time to time he could hear the children jabbering away with Thea in the kitchen. Curious, he went and stood near the kitchen door where he could observe his wife and his grandchildren, unseen.

Miriam and Benji, garbed in shorts, T-shirts, and sneakers, were sitting side by side on stools at the kitchen counter. Both were sawing away with crayons in their *Star Wars* coloring books. Thea, wearing a blue warm-up suit, was preparing a picnic lunch for the family to take to Margaretville where there was to be a Fourth of July carnival. Disliking the shrillness of carnivals, Gabriel had excused himself, pleading a stomach upset.

Suddenly Benji, who was covering Darth Vader with violet, piped out, "I love you best in the world, Grandma! You're prettier than Princess Leia!" Thea smiled in bliss.

After the others left for the carnival, Gabriel went to the bedroom and lay down. Beyond the window the waterfall roared. He fell asleep.

Young Gabe stands in the noon heat, a sheet drenched in urine over his head. They are punishing him because he wet his bed the night before.

Only he knows that it was really Toby Myers who peed in the bed. But he can't accuse Toby whom nobody sees. Now he must stand in the open, Toby's shame draped over his head. He smells the fumes. He sees the disc of the sun through the fabric of the sheet. He hears the taunts of the others; they include his brother, Michael, Jake, Hazel, and Toby Myers. He especially resents Toby's jeering: *Gabe peed his bed! Gabe peed his bed!* He must stand there, forbidden to move, while the sun bakes the sheet dry. He begins to cry with the humiliation he feels. Every night he lies awake, afraid to sleep, because he fears that Toby will wet the bed. Every night at bedtime he begs God not to let it happen tonight. But nothing works. He wakes every night just too late, feeling with horror the warm wetness flooding around him, soaking him, aware of what it is but unable to stop the flow in midcourse even though he knows that the next day he will have to stand in the sun with the sheet over his face, smelling the stink, enduring the laughter of Toby and the others. And on this day, as young Gabe stands there beneath the sheet, his shame turns to fury. His soul seethes with anger at his own helplessness, his own inability to do anything but endure. He hates the kids who taunt him—especially Toby Myers.

Gabriel woke to the sound of thunder. Beyond the bedroom window the hemlocks swayed in the wind. The smell of the pee-soaked sheet still filled his nostrils. *Another memory dream,* he thought, *a nightmare really, a reaction to Michael's dying.* But maybe these dreams had another provenance as well: his boy-self in search of … what? Release? All at once, as if borne on the approaching storm, an intuition seized Gabriel: something bad had happened out there in Missouri. He had to call Vonnie. Now! With the boom of thunder reverberating through the house, he went into the study and dialed.

"Hello?" A woman's voice but not Vonnie's rasp.

Gabriel said, "Who's this?"

"Mona."

Yes, Mona, Michael's daughter, the eldest of his children. Gabriel tried to recall what he knew of this Mona. He only knew that she was married, a mother, lived in Oklahoma, and taught at some college. She must have come down to West Plains from her own home to be with her father and help Vonnie. He identified himself to her.

"Uncle Gabe." She sounded amazed that he actually existed. "I'll get Vonnie."

Yvonne came on the line. "Gabe. I was going to call you a little later." She sounded exhausted, her voice a whisper. "Michael's very bad, near the end now. He's hallucinating and can't talk clearly. He thinks he's back in Woodstock with you."

Gabriel thought, *Maybe he is. Maybe Michael and I have been there together in our dreaming.*

Yvonne said, "The doctor thinks he might go any time now."

Gabriel groped for words to comfort her. "At least Michael and I were able to talk a couple of times. You know, about being kids together. It brought us closer, I think. Made him happy."

He really wanted to tell her how sorry he was that Michael and he had drifted apart, wanted to explain that they had all run away, not only he and Michael but Beth too. The three of them had sought new lives away from their past, and in running from that they had lost each other as well. But a stone of grief clogged Gabriel's throat and made it impossible for him to utter these thoughts.

Vonnie said, "Will we be seeing you at the funeral, Gabe?"

The funeral. Of course he would attend. How could he not?

She said, "I'll let you know when the end comes. So you can make travel plans."

How stoical she was. But of course she had to be. Somebody had to deal with the day-to-day.

She said, "Would you let Beth know what's happening? Save me a call?"

"Sure." They said good-bye.

Having now received the news that confirmed his intuition, Gabriel found himself entering into a state of tranquility, as if some part of him was imposing calm to keep from drowning in grief. The stone in his throat dissolved. As the storm broke outside he called Beth in Seattle and told her about Michael's deterioration.

She sounded as calm as he did himself. "Well, it's horrible but no shock. And he did redeem himself in the end."

Redeem himself? What did she mean?

Before he could frame the question, she said, "There's a lot you don't know about Michael, Gabe. He was an alcoholic. And he was a blowhard too, always telling tall tales and boasting when he was drunk."

Gabriel hadn't known, but he wasn't surprised. Booze and bullshit were in the Fallon genes.

Beth said, "And according to Vonnie, Michael could be violent too. To his kids and to her as well. I can personally testify that Michael had a lot of anger in him." She paused, as if considering whether to reveal more. She chose to go on. "A few years ago, when Michael was visiting me out here, he had too much to drink and slapped me in the face. Hard. The circumstances of the incident don't matter. I refused to speak to him again after that—until he got sick. Of course, since then I've forgiven him. Vonnie says he used to mistreat Olivia too."

Although he did not say so to Beth, Gabriel was surprised to hear that his brother, whom he remembered as self-effacing to the point of timidity, could explode in fury, as their father had so often. He would not have imagined Michael capable of such behavior. But what did it matter now?

Beth said, "The story gets brighter though. According to Vonnie, in these last years Michael fought off the boozing and the anger with her help. It was a struggle, but he became a figure in the community, even taught business courses at the local college. He learned how to be happy. Redeemed himself."

Gabriel asked her why she thought it important to pass this information on to him.

"I wanted you to know that Michael wasn't what he seemed." She hesitated and then said, "And neither am I."

"I'll remember that."

After hanging up with Beth, Gabriel made himself a vodka and tonic. The storm was still booming through the woods. The rest of the family were probably on their way home from the carnival. Drink in hand, he went to the bedroom. He sipped the vodka tonic, found it insipid, and put it aside on his dresser. At the rate his drinking was diminishing, he reflected, he might soon end up a teetotaler. Standing at the window, he stared out at the gloom where he could just make out the pillar of Eternity Falls. *So,* he thought, *Michael had had to fight his way past booze and wrath to achieve his life's goals.* This was even more reason for admiration. He resolved to say as much to Yvonne when he saw her at the funeral. He'd also let her know that he esteemed her for having rescued his brother from himself and that he admired her steadiness during Michael's decline. Despite his desire to express these sentiments to Yvonne, however, Gabriel quailed at the prospect of traveling to Missouri, of confronting her and the other strangers who were his brother's people. But he would force himself to do what he had to do.

It wasn't until they went to bed that night that Gabriel told Thea about the imminence of Michael's death. She turned over and embraced him. "It's better that it's come quickly, Gabe. I'll go with you, to the funeral I mean. The rest of the family can fend for themselves for a day or two." Gabriel knew that if Thea accompanied him to West Plains, she would contrive to soften the experience awaiting him there. This was her way—easing the path for those she loved. But this time Gabriel meant to face all of it head on.

"I have to go alone," he said. She nodded.

"Yes, I see. Yes, that's best for you to do it alone."

He said, "I'm hoping Michael will be able to hang on while the family's here. I really don't want to have to fly off during their visit."

"What will be, will be."

The following evening, Richard, ready for bed in slippers and navy pajamas, sprawled on one of the trio of couches that formed three sides of a square in the center of the living room. In jeans and a sweatshirt, Gabriel lounged in the wingback chair opposite him. They were alone. Everyone else had gone to bed after a day of hiking, fishing, and visiting with Ilse and Andrus. Tomorrow promised much activity too because Val was to arrive from the city.

Richard said, "I know I've disappointed you, Dad." Gabriel blinked in surprise. How was he supposed to reply to that statement? Denial? ("Of course you haven't disappointed me, Richard.") Wisdom? ("It's not me you have to please, Richard, but yourself.") The truth? ("Sure, you've disappointed me, Richard, as I've disappointed you. We all disappoint one another.") But Richard spoke again before Gabriel could utter any of these rejoinders. "I know my life seems odd to you, my profession unworthy, my faith bizarre. I'd like to explain myself, if I can." Gabriel tensed in anticipation of revelations from this son whose Fallon face masked a spirit that seemed very different from his own.

To encourage his son's mood, Gabriel said, "You can tell me anything, Richard. You know that. The fact is I've waited a long time for you to talk about yourself. You've become a sphinx over these last few years."

"Have I? I suppose I have. I'm sorry, but it's just that so much has happened to me that's hard to explain to other people—even you, Dad."

Gabriel inclined his head toward the glass wall where dusk had now turned to darkness. "We have all night."

"Okay then. Let me start by asking you this: do you have any idea why I gave up on medicine?"

The question promised a disclosure Gabriel longed to hear. He said, "You made some remark about not wanting to play God in a white coat."

Richard said, "It was really because of an emotion that has no name, or none I know about. For lack of a better term I call it spiritual disgust." He went on to say that he first experienced it at the start of his second year in med school. "I had just begun to appreciate the intricacy of the human body, the body I was educating myself to invade, to cut, to use. I was so awed that I kept asking myself how I, Richard Fallon, dared think myself worthy to interfere with the interplay of life and death. Yet I was surrounded by men and women who thought it their right to lord over life itself." He couldn't say exactly why, he went on, but the idea that mere mortals had the audacity to claim such power, to revel in it, appalled him. He soon became aware of the arrogance all around him. It repelled him so much that he found himself unable to function as his mentors demanded. The jargon, the coldness of the doctors, the complacency of the students, even the irreverence toward the cadavers, all of it nauseated him, often left him physically ill. "It came to me that if I didn't get out, I might become one of them. And so in disgust I left. I found that I couldn't explain myself, and so I didn't try. Later I came to realize that becoming a doctor was not part of God's plan for me. I was trying to do what I was not meant to do. And so my soul had sickened. But at that time, of course, neither Joyce nor I had found God's truth. I didn't really understand that there are a lot of ways to help people other than tending to their bodies. Spiritual ways. That knowledge only came later. Back then I only felt the disgust within me."

"And so you cured your revulsion against medicine by making money?"

"No. I can't say exactly why I went after money. Maybe it was in reaction to the false altruism I found in the medical profession. In finance there's no pretense. We admit that our goal is profit. I know it shocked you and Mom to see me in my Mercedes, throwing money around. It shocked me too—inside —the way Joyce and I both gorged on possessions. But I understand now that it was all part of God's script for us, just as my horror in med school was. When Joyce found the Lord and then brought me to him, I was ready. I had experienced the callous arrogance of science. I had submerged myself in the corruption of the money world. I had learned to play in the muck."

"But you also remained in the muck of the money world."

"To do God's will. And I stay in it to do God's will. That's my ambition now."

He went on to say that he and Joyce, in accordance with their reading of God's plan for them, had been giving away about half their family income every year, not only to their Holy Harbor Congregation before its demise but to charities as well. They also spent considerable sums on acts of kindness to individuals.

"I guess I want you to understand that even though I'm not a doctor but only a money grubber, I'm trying in my own way to do good."

"Are you and Joyce happy together?" Gabriel had long wanted to ask this question, for he had observed few signs of affection between Richard and Joyce. Of course he knew that the hottest fires often burn unseen. Still, he had to ask.

Richard answered without hesitation. "Joyce and I share a life, Dad. It's not like yours with Mom, full of storms and fire. We're not so demonstrative, not so—what? —passionate, I suppose. But we're happy in our pokey way. We believe that happiness derives from the certainty that God will point the way for us. It's very soothing to put yourself in God's hands."

Richard's reliance on a knowable, caring God seemed to Gabriel a risky strategy for life. Yet he was trying to make a deal with that same probably nonexistent God. Paradox was everywhere.

By now, as the Catskill night deepened, scores of light-mesmerized moths clung to the glass of the living room. Gabriel sensed he and Richard had reached that stage in their talk when the achievement of further intimacy required an exchange of vulnerabilities. He began the process by revealing to Richard his despair at failing to make himself a serious writer. He did not speak of the suicide sharks swimming within his brain, however, for he knew that to do so would burden Richard, as God's man, with the responsibility for saving his father from the pit. It would force Richard to resort to exhortation, guilt giving, and prayer—all to rescue his father from himself. Gabriel could not bring himself to lay that weight on Richard. Thus the suicide snakes remained a secret, even as he exposed the miscarriage that was his life.

When Gabriel finished, Richard's eyebrows rose in an expression of incredulity. "So you think you're a failure, Dad, despite a wonderful marriage and a loving family? Who are you to call your life a miscarriage? I know you're a skeptic, Dad, but God does have a script for each of us. Who's to say you won't write a great book yet? How do you know what lies ahead? If God wants a great book from you, it'll happen. And if not, it won't. There is no failure with God. No one has a right to despair."

Gabriel realized that his son, this man of faith, could never comprehend his exhaustion of spirit.

Richard said, "You know, Dad, I've fallen short of my own vision too. Everybody does."

Of course he is right, Gabriel thought. Everyone did fall short of their vision. But for most the death of the dream did not mean the death of the self. If for Richard there was no failure, for Gabriel there was nothing else. Only fear of the unknown and of causing pain to those he loved kept him groping after some kind of redemption, no matter how fantastic—in a waterfall's message perhaps, or in a fool's attempt to bargain with a God he didn't really believe in.

Richard said, "I know you're feeling depressed about Uncle Michael. But what's happening to Uncle Michael is only the end of his life on earth. His soul goes on. There's no real reason to mourn Uncle Michael."

Gabriel smiled into his son's earnest face. He wanted to say, "It isn't only Michael I'm mourning, kid. I'm also mourning the boys that Michael and I were all those years ago. I'm mourning the passage of time and the memories that still entangle Michael and me, and I'm mourning the man I wanted to become." But Gabriel knew he could never explain any of this to his son. He weighed telling Richard about the waterfall but discarded the notion. His Bible-bound son would probably interpret the phenomenon, if he credited it at all, as either an angelic epiphany or a demonic snare.

Richard said, "I would like to tell you, Dad, how I found my faith. It's a story only Joyce knows. I'm sure you'll think it very weird."

Gabriel leaned forward in anticipation of a revelation weightier than any he'd heard so far. "I'd be honored, Richard."

"The fact is that I resisted God for the longest time. I didn't just embrace the light after Joyce found the Lord. Though she tried to bring me to God, I wanted no part of it. She and I argued, or at least I did. I raged at her. She was an idiot. She was going insane. She was obsessed. She needed psychiatric help. I said all the things that nonbelievers say to derail a loved one's newfound faith. But Joyce only prayed for me. I threatened to leave her. Then one day something happened." He paused and grinned. "Promise you won't call me crazy, Dad?"

No chance of that, thought Gabriel. How could he, a man seeking words in a waterfall, a man who dreamed of his imaginary playmate of forty years ago, call Richard crazy? "Tell me the story, son."

"Okay. I was on an airplane. First class of course in those yuppie years. I was returning to O'Hare from Los Angeles. Late afternoon. The sun was streaming through the windows making golden circles on the seats and walls of the cabin." He halted yet again, as if recollecting the event. "I know this is going to sound awfully peculiar to you, Dad, but I swear to you, it's what happened."

"Go on."

"Well, the plane banked for the approach to O'Hare. The circles of light shifted to the ceiling. You know how they do when a plane's making that kind of turn. And then, I swear it, the plane stopped in midair and hung there. It seemed to me that time had stopped too. There was dead silence in the cabin. Not even engine noise. All the other people aboard were frozen like statues. Being the man I was then, I should have panicked, but I didn't. Instead I felt calm. I said, 'Lord, are you here?' In those days I would normally have felt embarrassed to utter those words, "Lord, are you here?" But at that moment I knew something important was happening, maybe the most important thing that would ever happen to me, but certainly something too important to be embarrassed about. I got up from my seat and struggled along the slanted floor back to the aft cabin. The passengers and the stewardesses were all frozen there as well, except for one bearded, youngish man occupying the aisle seat of the last row. He was dressed in ordinary jeans and a shirt. He smiled at me. I approached. He was beautiful, Dad. I don't mean pretty. He radiated light. It's hard to explain. Like an aura of glory. He spoke. His words are etched in my memory. 'Let me into your heart, Richard. Love me as Joyce does.' I knelt on the tilted floor, Dad, because it felt natural to do so. He put his hand on my head in blessing. 'In the grace of the Father is life everlasting,' he said. His exact words. I'll never forget them. I felt joy flood into me. Indescribable. And I knew I would never again be the man I was. 'I believe in you,' I said. And then I felt his peace in my soul. For the first time, Dad, I really knew I had a soul. 'You are my son,' he said. And then he was gone. The plane was banking once more, the passengers talking, the engines droning. I was still on my knees. The seat before me was empty. The flight attendants came running, thinking I'd fallen. They told me I should be in my place up front with my seatbelt fastened. I couldn't help laughing. Their worry seemed so absurd after what I'd just experienced. I went back to first class. I haven't been the same since, Dad. That experience taught me God is real and he dwells in me. Maybe you think it's delusion, but it's grace, Dad. Words can't express the enormity of the feelings involved, or make clear the shift that took place within me. But I was, literally, reborn. I don't expect you to accept it, Dad, but I've wanted to tell you this story for years. Maybe now you'll get a glimmer of why I feel so safe with God, why I trust his plan for me, why I know that with God there is no failure and no death."

They fell silent, as if both of them thought further talk superfluous. To Gabriel his son seemed at once more alien than ever—and more worthy of the love he felt for him. Father and son rose and, for the first time in more than a decade, embraced. Then they adjourned, each of them grateful to have spoken so much truth to the other.

Later, Gabriel wrote in his journal.

> Still no sign that God means to make me a serious writer in exchange for my believing in him. This is probably because God doesn't exist or can't be known to human beings. Whatever the case, I don't intend to make the mistake of bringing God into existence by wishful thinking. This, I fear, is what happened with Richard in the airplane. Some part of him craved peace with Joyce so much that it created a simulacrum of Christ among the tourist-class passengers. Isn't that also what happened to me with Toby Myers? But I was only a boy when I created my imaginary friend, if the word "create" truly describes how Toby came into being. Richard, however, is a full-grown man, not entitled to be humored for childish delusions. But who am I to point the finger at my son, I who have resurrected Toby Myers in my dreams, I who seek to decipher words in falling water? Moreover, who knows? Maybe Christ did appear in the plane, summoned by Richard's need of him. Mystery is everywhere if we would open our eyes to

it. And that comes from a man who is more sober these days than he has been in weeks.

Gabriel stopped writing. He remembered Michael's suggestion that as a writer he should approach the mystery of God by means of the written word. He resumed.

Maybe God is waiting for me to write him directly in this notebook. I'll have to think about that. In the meantime, whatever I may be hearing in the waterfall, I'm beginning to doubt I'm hearing the words of God. Surely if there is a God, he'd want to make himself understood, wouldn't he? He wouldn't hide in a waterfall and spout riddles like some oracle out of Greek myth, would he? He's too far beyond comprehension to play at such games, isn't he? Of course I might have to change my mind on that score, depending on what I find when I submit myself to Eternity Falls. And if it's not God in the waterfall, what is it?

CHAPTER 8

J UST AS THEA BEGAN serving the after-dinner coffee, Gabriel looked up
from his seat at the dining-room table and saw his daughter Valerie.
Duffel bag in hand, she was standing, unnoticed by the others, in the
doorway leading from the kitchen. She put a forefinger to her lips, warning
Gabriel against revealing her presence. She was dressed in jeans, sandals,
a red T-shirt that barely contained her ample breasts, and dark glasses.
Smiling at Gabriel as if the two of them had conspired at the drama of her
entrance, Valerie set her bag on the floor. She removed the glasses, brushed
strands of her hair off her face, and announced her arrival. "Can a poor
waif get a cup of coffee in this joint?"

Shouts of welcome greeted her. Val joined the others at the table. The
children saluted her with a tempest of energy. Benji climbed onto her lap
as she accepted a cup of coffee from a beaming Thea. Miriam took a post
at the side of Val's chair where she stared in adoration at her exciting aunt
who lived in New York and traveled the world. The children peppered her
with questions: Would she like to go catching frogs in the stream? Could
she play Pictionary with them? Would she tell them more about Africa
where she'd traveled on a field trip? Had she brought her violin with her?
Meanwhile the adults managed to exchange greetings and Thea, assuming
her mantle of motherhood, extracted from Valerie the fact that she wasn't
hungry, had eaten a burger on the road, and was "so glad" to escape the
city for a few days.

In the midst of the tumult Gabriel eyed this daughter of his. In spite of the stress of her lonely life in the city, she seemed to have donned a bright mask for the occasion of her visit. At this moment she reminded Gabriel of the golden girl she had been. He caught her eye with a smile. She responded with a wink of amusement, reminding Gabriel of the laughing Val that he had loved beyond expression in days gone by.

Hours later after everyone else had gone to bed, Val and Gabriel sat up talking and sipping Scotch in the living room. Although Gabriel's drinking had diminished to near abstinence by now, it had not in fact reached that point yet.

Father and daughter faced each other across a coffee table. She was barefoot, legs tucked up under her on the same couch where Richard had lounged. She wore a Columbia sweatshirt of light blue and black jeans. Gabriel had made himself comfortable in a white-collar shirt and running shorts. Feet propped on the table, he slouched in his wingback chair.

Val, her earlier vivacity now ebbing, began by telling him that she was thinking of giving up the chase for her doctorate. "I've been taking a good look at myself, Dad. The truth is that I don't find science all that consuming anymore. The stuff I do, what does it mean? I don't really give a shit about the incidence of diabetes among lowland gorillas. I don't burn with ambition to carry the torch of zoology up Kilimanjaro. The truth is I want a life. I'm no Curie or Margaret Mead. Let's face it—these last few years have proven that as a scientist I'm a dud."

In Gabriel's eyes she became for a moment the incandescent teenager of old. How many times had she come to him troubled? How many times had they talked like this? He'd been able to advise her then. That girl had respected his experience, but not anymore. The woman opposite him now only wanted him to listen, perhaps to comment. She no longer welcomed any offering of his wisdom, if wisdom he possessed—which he doubted, considering the disarray in his own life. And so he held his tongue and waited for her to go on.

She said, "There's another reason for bailing out, Dad. I think I'm in love."

Gabriel's heart sank. Love that ended in disaster had marred much of Val's adult life so far. He recalled in particular a liaison that had taken place seven years ago. Val, still an undergraduate then, though already twenty-three (she had delayed her entry into college for two years in favor of travel in Africa and Asia), had fallen in love with a professor of anthropology then in midcareer. The man, despite ambitions that militated against such recklessness on the gossipy campus where he taught, had left his pregnant wife to live with Val. Inevitably the business had collapsed in explosions of wrath, recrimination, and grief involving all three parties to the affair. The wife had forgiven the man, David, and he had fled back to her. Wounded, Val had taken refuge in a frenzy of work and self-loathing. Since that episode she had fallen twice more, to Gabriel's knowledge, into the quicksand. He had dared to warn her against the dangerous liaisons she seemed to favor, only to run up against her iron will and only to discover that she felt his advice as a reprimand. He had learned his lesson with Val: listen and say little.

She resumed speaking, her voice low. "It's a woman I'm talking about, Dad, and this time it's not one of my crazy flights. It could be the genuine article this time."

Gabriel took her news without blinking an eye. It was not for him to offer judgment on a matter he knew nothing about. And who could tell? Maybe this time she would find the love she longed for. She asked him to keep the information from Richard and Joyce. "When I'm ready I'll let them know. I just can't deal with any biblical condemnation right now."

Gabriel agreed. Then, in defiance of experience, he offered her a morsel of advice, perhaps only to demonstrate his concern for her. "Just don't jump into the fire to get out of the frying pan, Val. Consider well before you commit." Innocuous cliché. She sighed, but whether from weariness or in exasperation at his admonition, he couldn't tell.

Val finished her whiskey and changed the subject. "Ma tells me you're depressed these days. You've even stopped writing. What's up?"

Gabriel knew the futility of trying to evade her question—she'd only keep after him—so he gave her the account of his troubles that he'd already given Richard. This time, however, he concluded the recital with an addition. "I'm even hearing things in the waterfall."

Instantly intrigued, she said, "Hearing what things? Come on, Dad, give."

Well, why not? Test her reaction. Unlike Richard, she might comprehend his absorption with Eternity Falls. Though she professed atheism and trusted in science while Richard believed in miracles and advocated the divine, Val was far more open to mystery than her brother. Thus Gabriel now recounted for her his experience with the cataract, concluding with his plan to immerse himself in it in order to extract its message, if any.

When he finished, Val said, "What a wonderful idea!"

"Quirky anyway."

"No, no! Don't you see? Going under the falls is some kind of rite of passage."

"To what?"

"Who knows? To new growth maybe. At the risk of indulging in a burst of psychologizing, Dad, let me say that I think you've concocted the waterfall thing as an act of symbolism, something you've set up in your own mind to get you through this rough patch in your life. What you hear in the falls could be a message from your unconscious."

He couldn't help smiling. Despite her disclaimer about psychologizing, she had to cobble together a thesis for curing her dad's despair. It was how her mind worked. So typically Val. He almost apprised her of his skirmishing about with the question of God, but he thought better of it. That segment of his craziness would only earn her scorn. She would regard it as a symptom of grief over Michael's decline—or perhaps some reaching out for comfort. No, just as he'd withheld the waterfall story from Richard, he would now keep the God part of it from Valerie.

Valerie said, "What does Ma think about your waterfall thing?"

"I haven't told her. I'll let her know everything when the time's right. So don't say anything to her or to Richard either. Okay?"

She nodded. He knew he could trust her. She kept her word.

They were quiet for a while. Gabriel watched the moths batter against the glass in yearning—a paradigm of his life.

Val said, "Ma told me about the invitation to go to Chicago. Don't do it, Dad. You won't be able to endure Joyce's daffiness about all those demons and angels."

Gabriel thought, *If I find God in the waterfall, maybe Joyce won't seem so daffy.*

Gabriel woke up grumpy the next morning. Sunlight streamed through the bedroom window. He could hear the waterfall pounding beyond the glass. He recalled Val's suggestion of the night before that immersion in the cataract could lead to some kind of renewal. A neat concept. But on this morning the ordeal under the falls seemed more likely to drown him or send his heart into a fatal tachycardia. Still he would not evade the test under the cataract. When would he do it? Something would tell him when. In the meantime, he'd watch and wait and say nothing of all this to Thea.

Later Gabriel wrote in his journal.

With Michael still hanging on to life, I'm spending my time with Richard, Valerie, Joyce, and the children—all of us together, a rare event. As the days go by, however, my dread of going to Missouri for Michael's funeral increases. I shrink from facing the quietus of Michael's death and all the recollected pain it stirs up. But of course I will do it. By myself.

Still no sign from God. Maybe Michael was right in recommending that I write to him. A proposal? Maybe since I am not a believer God prefers, even requires, a written overture from me. Why not? Who am I to balk at such a formality? And so, here it is, my official proposition to God: By way of preamble, God, let me state for the record that I try not to whine. I'm well aware that your world abounds with people in agony, and I wish you'd explain that one to us down here! Still I find myself in dire straits—black thoughts, bad memory dreams, fantasizing about the waterfall. If you're real, you know it all. In summary, I'm feeling about as lost as I've ever felt and pretty desperate as well.

Otherwise I don't think I'd be trying to get in touch with you, because even now, as bad as I feel, I can't bring myself to believe in your existence. I mean I can't believe that you exist in any form I can grasp—unless it's you I hear in the waterfall. Anyway, I want to believe in you. I'm ready to embrace whatever faith is, if you're willing to show yourself to me in some unambiguous way. So, here's the deal, God: Give me your grace, as Richard would put it, and I'll give you whatever you require in return—belief, worship, whatever. I realize that my proposal is more than a little inelegant and no doubt presumptuous as well. I apologize for that. I also realize I haven't spelled out my proposition in detail, but that doesn't matter, does it? You're no trickster who employs legalese. You're omniscient after all. You know full well what I mean by this offer. So there it is, God. If you exist, let's talk. You've got a week to get back to me. That should be more than enough.

Gabriel anticipated no reply from the Almighty. But on the other hand, nothing ventured, nothing gained.

Valerie cornered Gabriel in the kitchen after lunch as he sat alone with a glass of cranberry juice. "I've got to talk to you, Dad. Something important. Come get the mail with me." She took his arm and led him out of the house to the driveway. They set off toward the road and the mailbox.

Gabriel felt his heart bumping around. She had something important to tell him. Had Michael died?

Finches and jays, flashes of color, were flitting about under the hemlocks. Suppressing his alarm, Gabriel walked in silence with his daughter. They stopped on the stone bridge where the driveway crossed the flow downstream from Eternity Falls. They stared down at the trout hanging in the shadows beneath the arch of the span.

Valerie said, "When Benji and I were out observing tadpoles this morning, he was chattering on as he usually does with me, and he began to talk about something I found disturbing. He said that he and an eleven-year-old boy from next door, Darryl, have been playing games that involve sexual touching and maybe worse."

Gabriel's heart flopped like a beanbag. Little Benji. Was Benji to pay the price of Richard and Joyce's mission in the city?

"I wanted to get you alone so I could tell you. I haven't even breathed this to Ma. What do you think we should do?"

Gabriel found himself wondering if Benji's Darryl might be his grandson's version of Toby Myers. "Any chance that Benji's making up a story?"

"What six-year-old kid knows enough to make up something like that?"

Of course the boy hadn't made up the story. Nevertheless, Gabriel wanted to hear about these games from Benji's own lips before going any further. He told Valerie as much and she agreed.

An hour later Gabriel contrived to be alone with Benji over milk and cookies in the kitchen. Assuming his persona as gruff grandfather, he asked his grandson a direct question. "Can other people see this kid, Darryl?"

Benji laughed. "Oh, Grandpa, that's silly."

Gabriel asked what games he and Darryl played. Benji hesitated for a second then repeated the tale he'd told to Valerie. As Gabriel interrogated the boy further, he saw that Darryl had initiated their play and that Benji had participated out of innocence. Still Benji did seem to sense something not quite right about these games, for he hadn't mentioned them to his mother and father or to Miriam. Or, Gabriel told himself, perhaps only one or two incidents had occurred—too few to make more than a superficial impression on the boy.

Certainly the episodes with Darryl seemed to have left Benji unaffected, for he spoke of them without shame. But only an expert could determine if Benji had suffered damage. In the meantime Gabriel needed to communicate the story to Richard and Joyce so they could take steps to protect Benji. But how to report it?

After dinner, when the Midwest Fallons had gone to bed, Gabriel sat up with Valerie and Thea, who had by now heard the tale from Val, to determine how to break the news. They agreed that Gabriel should act as the messenger and that he should impart the information to Richard the following morning when he and Richard were planning to cart a load of trash to the Margaretville Collection Station.

CHAPTER 9

FTER BREAKFAST RICHARD AND Gabriel left for the dump with a Jeep-ful of refuse. On the way Gabriel told the tale of Benji's encounters with the neighbor boy. Richard, his face white with shock and anger, listened without interruption until Gabriel finished. Then he expelled a chestful of air and stared at the passing pastures, their green relieved here and there with sprays of goldenrod. His hands, resting in his lap, kept flexing into fists.

At last Richard said, "It couldn't be just a fib?" He answered his own question. "No, of course not. Little kids don't make up stuff like this. Lord God! Poor Benji." He slammed his right fist into the palm of his left hand. "This is Joyce's fault! I don't know how many times I've told her she has to supervise our kids more closely. She's too trusting. She has no street smarts."

Gabriel suspected that much of Richard's wrath was derived from his own sense of guilt. After all he had acted as Joyce's partner in exposing the children to the squalor in which their parents had chosen to live. Moreover, Richard often had to travel on business, leaving Joyce and the children home alone to cope with the hazards rampant in their neighborhood.

As if talking to himself, Richard said, "The thing now is to protect Benji against whatever's been happening. The neighborhood's improving, but it's still full of kids like Darryl, raised by irresponsible elders, sexualized by the behavior they see around them, all the abuse, the drugs, the violence.

I thought I detected something a little bent about this Darryl kid. I can feel sorry for him, but I don't want him near Benji. Never again."

At the dump Gabriel and Richard, laboring in silence, tossed bags of garbage into the hole, emptied glass bottles and tin cans into bins, and stacked old copies of the *Times* in a shed that smelled of rot. When they started for home again, a glowering Richard said, "This is a warning from God. Joyce has to develop a more realistic picture of the environment we've taken our kids to. She has to understand that she has to supervise Benji better. She has to shed her naïveté. We can't let Benji suffer for our work."

Gabriel thought it unfair that Richard was putting so much blame on Joyce, but he held his tongue. Benji was their son. It was their responsibility to protect him, and they had to choose their own method.

Back at the house Gabriel parked the Jeep and went up to the study where he began to record in his journal an account of Benji and the sex games. At one point he looked out the window and spotted Richard and Joyce sitting together on a bench placed at the edge of the stream. Richard, gesturing vehemently, was doing the talking. Joyce, paler than usual, was staring at him. Suddenly she rose from the bench. She ran from her husband, back toward the house, as if to escape his accusations. Moments later Gabriel heard the guest-room door slam out in the hallway. He supposed that Joyce had taken refuge there, had flung herself on the bed to sob forth her shock and misery. He peeped out into the hallway. To his surprise, he saw Thea letting herself into the guest room. Curious, he went and stood by the closed door. He could hear the two voices within.

"Richard puts everything on my shoulders." This was Joyce between sobs.

Thea responded. "I know. It's not fair." Gabriel pictured Thea, a goddess of sympathy, seated alongside Joyce on the bed, her arm around the younger woman.

Joyce again. "He's always gone on business. I might as well be a single mom. The whole burden of the household, the children, the Holy Harbor problems, all the daily mess—it all falls on me. I try, Thea! Honest I do. But I can't do everything myself! If it weren't for the Lord's help, I'd never be able to hold myself together—and now this awful thing done to Benji! I feel I'm falling apart!"

"This isn't about you, Joyce; it's about Benji. You and Richard have to work together now to help your son."

"Yes. You're right." A paroxysm of sobbing ensued on the other side of the door. Feeling a twinge of shame for eavesdropping, Gabriel crept back to the study.

That afternoon when he went down to the kitchen to make himself a sandwich, Gabriel encountered Thea. She was brewing a pot of tea for herself. Slapping ham on rye bread, Gabriel said, "Everything okay with Joyce?"

"I got her calmed down. She's sleeping now. Richard blamed her for the episodes with Benji. His criticism upset her terribly. She let loose some pent-up emotions."

"I heard a little of it. I was listening at the door for a while."

Thea lifted an eyebrow in disapproval. "Well, then you know Joyce feels overwhelmed in spite of her God." She poured a cup of tea and sipped. "I suggested that she and Richard make time to reignite old flames. You can't live without the physical elements of love, I told her." She took another sip of tea. "I doubt she'll take my advice. Probably she'll just pray. Anyway they have to sail their own ship." She smiled, and Gabriel thought—not for the first time—how much iron there was in her, along with the kindness and beauty.

Later Richard pulled Gabriel aside and reported that he'd talked at length with Benji and had concluded that only one or two incidents had taken place with the neighbor boy. "And it won't happen again. Joyce and I plan to keep Benji away from Darryl. This was a wake-up call from God."

"Are you and Joyce okay?"

"She was pretty upset. I guess I was a little hard on her. But we're okay now." He paused then said, "You know, Dad, sometimes I'm tempted to go out on the streets and start dispensing justice myself, but then I remember that God is going to take care of all that in the end."

Gabriel thought, *My bible-thumping son, I only hope he's right.*

That night as Thea and Gabriel prepared for bed, the phone in the bedroom rang. He picked it up. Beth was on the line: "Gabe? I've just heard from Vonnie that Michael's fallen into a coma. I told her I'd let you know."

He took the news calmly. "Well, we've been expecting this, haven't we?'

Beth said, "I've decided to leave for Missouri tonight. I want to be there when Michael dies, even if he doesn't know it. What are your plans?"

He had no plans. He said, "Richard and Joyce are going home the day after tomorrow. I'll fly out to Missouri right after that, unless the end comes before then, of course." He added that Thea would remain in Margaretville.

Beth said, "Were you able to take care of any unfinished business with Michael?"

Gabriel wondered what she meant by the question. Just an example of her psych talk? Or was she implying that he might have needed to deal with some problem between Michael and him, such as the patching up of a quarrel? If so she had missed the mark. No such breach existed. Although Michael's family might resent Gabriel for his neglect, Michael and he had never been enemies. They had been strangers. He assured Beth that he and Michael had shared their memories at the end.

Beth said, "I'm glad. I'll see you in the Ozarks."

In bed Gabriel and Thea lay side by side in the dark. They made love and fell asleep. Gabriel dreamed, not of his brother, but of dancing with Thea under the waterfall. When he woke he could remember little of the dream, just that it had given him pleasure. Lying in bed, with the sun streaming across the covers, he resolved that he would try not to think of Michael's dying on this last day of Richard and Joyce's visit. That grief would engulf him again soon enough.

The day turned into a festival outdoors. In the afternoon, after much splashing and hilarity in the stream, Thea and Gabriel chose teams—Valerie, Miriam, and Joyce on Gabriel's side; Richard and Benji on Thea's—for a game of touch football on the lawn. With a sarcasm that recalled his pre-airplane–conversion personality, Richard said, "Shades of Camelot." Thea's team won, ten touchdowns to nine, because Miriam and Joyce, Gabriel's teammates, had no facility whatever for catching a football.

Following the game, as the shadows crept out of the woods, Richard built a fire in back of the house and set about cooking burgers and hot dogs. The kids raced about while the adults watched from chairs by the fire.

After eating, and with dusk deepening by the minute, the children and Valerie set out to catch fireflies in jars. As Gabriel observed this changeless pastime he found himself reliving a memory from his own childhood. He was back again in twilight on the lawn of the Keller house. He was chasing fireflies along with Michael, Jake Keller, and Hazel. With the rise of a half-moon, Jake and Hazel went off and lay down together behind a blackberry bush. Michael flung himself onto the grass to stare at the stars as they emerged. Knowing his role on these occasions, young Gabe took up his position as lookout near the bush where Jake and Hazel were now making out. He watched by the light of the moon as Jake kissed Hazel and held her close. This arousing yet warm and tender recollection vanished when Richard's voice reached Gabriel across the fire.

"It's been a marvelous visit, Dad, despite the scare about Benji. We'll all be sorry to leave tomorrow."

Gabriel nodded. Richard had to be in Los Angeles Monday to close a deal for some amusement park investors. He had laughed in telling about it. "Millions of dollars for a stupid roller coaster while people go hungry in Bucktown. No wonder my business leaves me cold." Richard said he and Joyce planned to get away about noon the next day in order to arrive in Newburgh in time for their flight to Chicago.

Gabriel said, "Are you and Joyce really okay?"

"We're fine."

As darkness gathered, stars began to glitter overhead. The children gave up their firefly chasing. Everyone drew together around the fire. Thea and Joyce fetched jackets from the house for everybody. They roasted marshmallows. Benji insisted on burning his black and eating the skin with his fingers.

Miriam made a face. "Ugh!"

In response Benji opened his mouth and stuck out his tongue to display a gooey remnant of marshmallow.

Miriam cried out in mock horror. "You're gross!"

Delighted that he had inspired disgust in his sister, Benji shrilled with laughter.

In the intervals of silence Gabriel could hear Eternity Falls roaring upstream. Would he ever find the courage to give himself up to that frigid and ceaseless torrent?

Later as night settled in, Thea and Joyce packed the kids off to bed despite Benji's protests. The adults, braving the chill, hunched their chairs around the fire.

Suddenly Joyce said, "Would this be a good time to tell about the demise of Holy Harbor?" Thea answered for all of them. "Definitely."

Joyce stared into the fire as if mustering her thoughts. Her yellowish eyes seemed to flare like a cat's in the light. She took a breath and launched into her tale.

"You all know that we set up Holy Harbor Congregation on instructions from the Lord." Joyce paused, allowing her listeners a moment to absorb the sanctity of this mission—and thus the cosmic import of what she was about to disclose. She went on. "Oh, I know you all don't believe—especially you, Valerie—and that's okay. Whether you believe it or not, it's true that God wanted us to establish Holy Harbor. What's not true is the story that Holy Harbor came apart simply because the people in it fell into disagreement among themselves. The truth is that Holy Harbor was overthrown by the devil. A spiritual battle was fought over Holy Harbor and the devil's army won because too many of us in the church failed to fight the demons that came against us."

Again Joyce halted, gazing into the fire's glow as if beholding in the coals a replay of the battle for Holy Harbor. Gabriel knew that she meant her listeners to take her tale literally. For her the devil was no allegory.

Joyce resumed. "The Lord allowed me to see the servants of evil fighting nightly with the soldiers of God for possession of Holy Harbor. He permitted me to hear the clashing of spiritual swords, the screaming of souls in peril, and the foul cursing of the demons within the walls of Holy Harbor. I was the only one who actually saw and heard those spiritual battles. Even Richard was unable to perceive them, though his faith told him they were there and he fought, as I did, with prayer, prayer, and more prayer."

Valerie interrupted. "You really saw these demonic battles? With your eyes?"

"With my spiritual eyes, yes."

"What does that mean, spiritual eyes?"

Joyce looked up from the fire and gave Val a smile of forbearance. "It's hard to explain. You don't just see the demons all at once. You sort of sense them first. You're somehow aware of their presence. You begin to feel their evil around you. You hear them. Even smell them sometimes. Then, if the Lord allows, you begin to distinguish their forms. Finally when your spiritual eyes are fully open, you see them bodily, as they would appear on our earth."

Valerie said, "What did they look like?"

"The ones I saw were shaped like big lizards, worms, and hissing reptiles."

"Could they fly? Like the monkeys in *The Wizard of Oz*?"

Thea broke in. "Let Joyce tell the story, Val."

Joyce said, "Oh, I understand Valerie's doubts. But I'm not afraid to be mocked for the sake of the truth. I know what I saw, and I swear to you the Lord gave me eyes to see the demonic beasts hovering about Holy Harbor. At first I was terrified at the sight of them. But I prayed and—Praise God!—the Lord strengthened my heart so I could look upon them without flinching. And the Lord told me that we of Holy Harbor could only drive them away with prayer. But that was where we fell short, because the pastor we had chosen to lead us was blind. Our congregation couldn't unite in prayer, couldn't muster the spiritual strength to drive off the invaders of the House of the Lord."

Across the fire, Gabriel caught Valerie's eye. She lifted her eyebrows as if to say, "This woman is crazy." Shifting his attention to Richard, Gabriel saw that he was regarding Joyce with an expression of serenity on his face. Gabriel surmised that, even if Richard hadn't seen Joyce's devils, he shared her belief that the forces of hell had waged war against Holy Harbor Congregation. Gabriel looked away into the darkness as Joyce continued her account of the spirit war that, to her mind, had brought down Holy Harbor.

"I felt that it was up to me as God's witness to rally my brothers and sisters against the evil ones. And so I described the demon beasts that were attacking Holy Harbor—attacks that my brothers and sisters could not even feel much less see. I pleaded for more prayer, more prayer, more prayer, always more prayer. But I found that my brothers and sisters didn't have it in them to believe the truth or to utter the prayers needed. In the end the forces of hell prevailed because we of Holy Harbor were too corrupt to support the angelic ones. There were times I could smell the corruption. And I knew that Holy Harbor would be destroyed because of human corruption."

Here Joyce stopped, done with her story of devils and angels at war.

Valerie broke the ensuing hush. "But surely there was more to it than that. Earlier you spoke of dissension. Tell us about that part of it."

Joyce resumed. Now her narrative revolved about church politics and pastoral disagreements. Gabriel soon concluded that, in spite of Joyce's assertions that an epic spiritual struggle had brought down Holy Harbor Congregation, in reality an all-too-human contest for dominance had caused its fall.

In essence, and putting aside Joyce's fantasy, the story came down to this: Pastor Tom had insisted that his will prevail within the congregation even though Richard paid the bills and the minister had agreed prior to taking the job that a congregation council would make the decisions within the assembly. Having tasted the sweetness of power, as Joyce put it, Pastor Tom had declared himself leader of the congregation, in charge of all he surveyed. Joyce said, "He was seduced by the devil." Eventually Richard had called for a meeting of the membership to determine how Holy Harbor was to operate. According to Joyce it was this act that precipitated the spiritual war for possession of the Lord's house.

In the temporal world of humanity, however, the struggle became a conflict with bureaucracy. Pastor Tom not only opposed holding a meeting of the congregation, he also appealed in secret for support to his superior in the hierarchy of his denomination. The church official backed the pastor.

He even wrote a letter in which he denounced Richard as a "maker of discord." Pastor Tom, without informing Richard in advance, read this letter to the Holy Harbor Congregation during a Sunday service.

Shaking her head as if the memory of Pastor Tom's perfidy still had the power to shock her, Joyce said, "That was the devil speaking from our pastor's mouth."

In the aftermath, Richard and Joyce, counseled by God, had withdrawn from Holy Harbor Congregation. Without Richard's money to support it, the church-cum-shelter had soon closed its doors.

Her face reflecting the last glow of the fire, Joyce said, "But we still intend to stay in Chicago. The defeat at Holy Harbor is part of God's script for us. Now we're going to work in our own way. There's a lot to do, and we now know we can do it without the help of the church. There's a cloud of evil over the city of Chicago. As you know it has even touched our own son. We intend to help disperse that filthy cloud. Praise God!"

Again Gabriel observed the derision on Valerie's face. He hoped his own face did not reveal the disdain he felt for Joyce's cosmos, for despite the absurdity of her fixations, Gabriel had no desire to wound her with acts or words of scorn. And anyway, wouldn't most people think his fixations just as absurd as Joyce's? Wasn't he planning to bathe in the waters of Eternity Falls to decode a message? Hadn't he written to God?

With the completion of the Holy Harbor story, a silence fell over the group. The fire was turning to ashes. Richard yawned. Thea said, "Time for bed."

As Gabriel locked up the house, Valerie came up to him in the hallway. "Do you really think you can live in Chicago with that crazy woman, Dad? Demons and muttering lizards? Every other word followed by 'Praise God'?"

Gabriel thought of mitigating Valerie's harshness with a reminder of his own obsession with the waterfall. Before he could speak however, Valerie said, "I wonder if Richard really believes all Joyce's God bullshit. Do you suppose my very smart brother realizes she's crazy and he's just humoring her? No. He must believe that bizarre crap himself or he wouldn't risk his kids, would he? Man, people are grotesque, aren't they? I'll see you in the morning." She gave him a kiss on the cheek and went off to bed.

Gabriel made his way upstairs to the bedroom. Thea was already huddled down under the covers. He crawled in beside her and shut off the lamp.

A moment later he heard her murmur, "In spite of everything, Gabe—your depression, Michael's dying—it's been a wonderful visit with the children, and with Richard and Valerie. It's so seldom we have the whole family about us like this. I want to cherish it."

"And Joyce? What do you make of her? Valerie thinks she's crazy."

"I won't deny that her demon war and her cloud of evil over Chicago strike me as weird. But millions of people share her beliefs, don't they? She certainly has Richard persuaded, doesn't she? And he's no fool. Maybe we are the weird ones." She fell silent.

Outside in the darkness, Gabriel could hear the waterfall. The voice of God?

CHAPTER 10

G ABRIEL WOKE. THEA WAS asleep at his side. The bedroom clock read 2:33 a.m. As he lay in bed, hoping that sleep would reclaim him, his mind began to race. He pictured Michael breathing his last in the Missouri night that was the same night as the one in Margaretville, New York. He imagined his son and daughter, his grandchildren too, all abed in this house—and it came to him that Michael in his coma, and the others asleep nearby, were all alive and acting in his head. He thought how everyone lived in the minds of other people—as a memory, an image, a sound, a scent. In such forms, everyone in the world might live in thousands of other minds. Gabriel shivered at this conception, for it seemed to express, in a fashion that troubled him, the mystery embedded in every living being, the mystery it was impossible to describe let alone solve: what the soul might be and how it continues. If it continues.

Gabriel considered getting up and having a whisky. It might help him get back to sleep. But he soon thought better of it. He seemed to be losing his desire for booze, as if the bouts of drinking in the time of his crying jags had worn out his taste for alcohol. Thus, rather than get out of bed or dwell further on the mysteries of the soul, he sought a return to sleep by dredging up images from his memory: sailing under the stars, Venice at dusk, his first sight of the Himalayas at dawn. For once the trick worked. As his interior eye filled with a picture of sunlight upon the flank of a snow-laden mountain, Gabriel drifted again into unconsciousness.

A column of falling water appears before him. It foams white. But instead of rushing down, it falls slowly, slowly, murmuring, into the pool below. Its cloud of droplets hangs in the air, motionless. Gabriel knows this is a dream and the column of water before him is Eternity Falls.

He is naked. His skin is pale in the light that seems to come from no source he can discern. He stands at the base of the cataract and gazes at the water drifting before him. It creates a warm mist. The dampness bathes his naked body, the graceful body of his youth. Moisture soaks his hair. He feels it condensing on his skin.

As Gabriel stands within the fog, he hears the water whisper. He can't make out the words, but he knows they belong to a chain of beauty. A poem? A song? He can't tell. He edges closer to the veil of water. He sees a naked woman, a girl really, through the liquid curtain. Her hair is forest green. It reaches down her back in soaked strands. Her body, white as the moon, gleams with the water that bathes her. Foam clings to her breasts, slides down her arms, between her thighs. Gabriel knows she is the nymph of the falls.

The woman gestures, urging Gabriel to come to her through the drift of water. He understands that she is the waterfall, that the waterfall has chosen this form to represent its beauty. Perhaps she is also the singer of the song in the falling water. Again she signals Gabriel to come to her. He steps forward until he is standing under the water, but he feels nothing—not its weight, not its force, not its wetness. He steps through the curtain and finds himself in a grotto cut from the mountain by ages of scouring water. The nymph of the falls points to a moss-grown rock wall that glistens with moisture.

Gabriel tries to take the hand of the nymph, but the hand has no substance. The nymph shakes her hair, wringing from it a fountain of liquid. She points once more toward the mossy rock face. He understands that she has now assumed her role as the guardian of the gate. The wall of rock opens and the nymph evaporates like a cloud. The rock portal, gaping wide, invites Gabriel to enter. His heart beats against his ribs. Although he can see nothing but blackness ahead, he steps across the threshold.

He finds himself in space—a virgin universe. Slowly it fills with floating galaxies, glowing dust, and planets that glide out of pools of blackness. Gabriel hears a voice: "All this can be yours." The thumping of his heart grows more rapid. He looks up. Above him, hanging in the void as he is himself, Gabriel beholds another creature—this one as ugly as the nymph was lovely.

The creature has the appearance of a reptile, a male. A ragged crest runs the length of his green body, from triangular head to the tapering tail. Yellow-eyed, sharp-toothed, diamond-clawed, the creature's skin shimmers in the light of the galaxies. The bent legs grasp the emptiness and, against all the laws of nature, hold on to nothing.

The reptile, which Gabriel identifies as a demon, hisses. "There is no God, but all this universe can be yours if you will do the necessary." The creature swims away through the emptiness.

Gabriel shouts after it, "If I will do the necessary what?" A response reaches him from some source out in the void: a scream of laughter that Gabriel recognizes as issuing from the throat of Toby Myers.

Gabriel woke with the sun streaming into the room. Thea's side of the bed was empty. He lay on his back and stared up at the ceiling where a spider was running, first one way and then the other as if confused about where she'd left her web. As he watched the spider, Gabriel considered the dream that just ended. Like almost all his sleeping visions nowadays, this one of the nymph and the demon had unfolded with a movie-like coherence. Unlike his memory dreams, however, this one struck him as phantasm, unrooted in any reality. And yet it disturbed him as much as his memory dreams, for he sensed that this vision too carried with it a cargo of meaning. In an effort to explore this notion further, he reviewed its details. He saw again the nymph of the falls and the demon lizard. Might the dream have something to do with his letter to God, his unconscious commenting on the futility of it? Or perhaps it was only a manifestation of Joyce's account of the fall of Holy Harbor. The necessary—what did that mean? Ambiguity.

There was no use trying to unravel it, so he let the residue of the dream escape into oblivion and turned his attention to the day ahead. Richard, Joyce, and the children would be leaving for home after lunch. He would miss the warmth and the distraction their visit had provided. Still, they needed to return to their normal life. Normal life. Was any life normal? Certainly not Joyce's. And not his either.

After lunch, while Thea helped Richard and Joyce pack their car, Val took the children for a last romp in the stream while Gabriel watched from the bank. On this day the waterfall offered no words to tease his mind. Only the shouts of Miriam and Benji reached his ears and the laughter of his daughter, whose face gleamed in the sun and seemed intermittently to melt back into the face of the girl she had been.

Then it was time to go. Baggage was stowed in the Taurus. Hugs were given all around.

Richard said to Gabriel, "Come live with us in Chicago, Dad."

"I'm thinking about it." In fact he wasn't. He had too many other matters on his mind to worry about moving to Chicago.

Richard hugged him. "I love you, Dad."

Gabriel started to whisper to Richard that he loved him too, but Benji's shrieks of farewell intervened. Joyce reminded Richard that they had a plane to catch. Moments later, the Midwest Fallons drove off, the Taurus rocking up the driveway, the kids shouting and waving, until the car reached the road and passed out of sight.

Thea, Valerie, and Gabriel returned to the house. Miriam and Benji had taped a series of drawings to the wall of the living room: the Little Mermaid, Jabba the Hutt, and Princess Leia. The artists had signed their work in block letters. Gabriel let the pictures hang. Thea would enjoy looking at them from time to time.

An exhausted Thea soon fell asleep on the couch. Valerie's mood had darkened, as if she was thinking of the city and the future awaiting her there. She read a magazine in silence.

Gabriel stood before the living-room glass and stared out at the falls. He wondered if he could really endure a stay in Chicago, with children around all the time and Joyce with her demons at war with her biblical God. Praise God! Could he put up with *that* day after day?

It came to him that God had only four days left to respond to the deal he had proposed. So far Gabriel had detected no sign that God had even the slightest interest in making the deal.

The phone in the kitchen rang, blasting like a siren through the cavernous rooms. Gabriel, guessing what the ringing signified, answered.

The voice on the other end of the phone identified itself as Lawrence, Michael's son. "My dad died an hour ago."

Gabriel murmured some response. Not yet able to absorb the fact of Michael's death, he thought, *Lawrence, yes, Lawrence, voice of solemnity.* Which one of the sons is Lawrence? The doctor? Yes, the intern from New Orleans. ("I got all those kids through college. I accomplished what I set out to do.")

The young man on the phone, for whom Gabriel was Uncle Gabe, focused on the practical: the funeral would be Monday afternoon, the day after tomorrow, 4:00 p.m. Missouri time.

Lawrence, the doctor from New Orleans, Michael's son, said, "My father wanted the funeral ASAP. He was adamant about it, Uncle Gabe. My father could be stubborn. We want to honor his wishes. I hope you understand. I hope you'll be able to get here."

Gabriel assured him he'd get there and asked after Yvonne.

"She's holding up. She's a tough lady." The young man had no time to dawdle. No doubt he had to make a lot of these calls. Doing his duty, a stoic, filling in for Yvonne. "I look forward to meeting you, Uncle Gabe."

Did he detect an unspoken question wrapped in Lawrence's words? "What was it between you and my father Uncle Gabe that caused you to stay away from us for all these years?" But it didn't matter. Whatever Michael's family thought of him, Gabriel meant to travel to West Plains and take whatever he encountered there—contempt, anger, or reprimand.

After another expression of sorrow, Gabriel hung up. He found Thea and Valerie in the kitchen with him. They were staring at him, ready to offer help or sympathy—whatever he needed.

Still not grasping the fact, Gabriel thought, *Michael's dead, little Michael.* He said to Thea, "Funeral's Monday. I ought to fly out there tomorrow. That'll give me a day with his family."

Thea said, "I'll make the arrangements."

Gabriel went up to the bedroom. He looked out the window where the sun was turning the foam of Eternity Falls to ivory edged with gold. By now the Midwest Fallons would have arrived at Newburgh, might even have boarded the plane to O'Hare, Benji squirming in his seat.

His brother was dead. Little Michael was dead.

How was he to assimilate that? The boy he knew in Woodstock, Michael, his brother, had gone from this earth, and some of the oldest parts of Gabriel had gone with him. He thought, *What am I feeling at this moment?* A tide of sorrow. And something else: loneliness, a deprivation that nothing can fix. This was bereavement. Michael's death had recreated in Gabriel the loneliness of the abandoned child that had been him.

Gabriel vowed that in Missouri he would not only say farewell to Michael but also to his young self. Not only would he bury Michael, he would also heal that forsaken boy, himself, truly and at long last, forever.

Yeah, time to say good-bye, pal, but not to me. I just got here.

Gabriel recognized the voice inside his head as that of Toby Myers. So, Toby was no longer confining himself to dreams.

I'm back, pal; here to help you.

Gabriel found himself responding aloud, as he used to when Toby had accompanied young Gabe everywhere. "Where are you, Toby? Why are you hiding? Come out and let me see you."

Toby said, *All in good time, pal. Trust me. I'm your friend again.*

"A lot of water has flowed under the bridge, Toby. Have you changed much?"

Changed? Me? No. Never. But you sure have changed, pal.

"Show yourself, Toby. Let me see that twisted arm of yours."

Silence. Toby had departed—for a while. However, Gabriel knew Toby meant to return, but for what purpose?

As he continued to look out on the falls, Gabriel heard Thea come into the bedroom. He didn't turn around but kept his eyes fixed on the cascade.

A moment later he felt her pressing against him from behind, leaning her head against him. Her arms snaked around across his chest. He heard her voice: "You can't fly out tomorrow, Gabe. Nothing's available. So you'll have to fly out of Newburgh Monday morning at 5:00 a.m., a commuter flight to Philadelphia then TWA to St. Louis, and another commuter jump to Springfield, Missouri. The West Plains airport is too small for commercial flights."

Gabriel said nothing. Thea detailed more of her arrangements for him: In Springfield he'd rent a car and drive two hours to West Plains, where she had reserved a room at the Best Western. "The funeral's at four so you should be okay for time."

He turned around and embraced her. Her head rested on his chest. For some reason he suddenly wanted to tell her about the waterfall. But intuition warned against it. She had enough on her mind right now. So did he.

Letting her go, Gabriel sat on the bed. He picked up the bedroom phone and punched in the West Plains number that he now knew by heart. He had expected a busy signal because of Vonnie receiving calls of sympathy from friends. Instead young Lawrence, all business, answered on the second ring. Gabriel gave him the information about his arrival Monday in time for the funeral.

"I'm sorry I can't get there earlier."

"I understand. But don't bother to rent a car. A friend of my dad's will be coming from Springfield to the funeral. She can give you a lift. Her name is Phyllis Tate. She'll find you at the airport."

Gabriel wrote "Phyllis Tate, airport" on the bedside pad. Then another voice replaced Lawrence at the other end: Beth. She'd flown in from Seattle the day before. "Michael was comatose when I got here. Still I'm glad I was on hand at the end." She was staying at a Ramada Inn in town. She expressed disappointment to find that Gabriel wouldn't arrive until the day of the funeral.

"Can't be helped."

Beth informed him that their cousin Kevin, an oil company executive, had flown up from Houston to attend the funeral. One of his company's

private jets had deposited him at the small airport in West Plains and would return for him after Michael's burial. Gabriel conjured up a picture of this cousin whom he hadn't seen in decades: a handsome young Fallon dressed in the blue uniform of the air force. When a teenager, Kevin—four years older than Gabriel—had been an outstanding scholar and athlete.

"A company plane, eh? I take it Kevin's a big shot."

Beth said, "Most definitely. He and Michael became friends at some business convention in Kansas City last year." She fell silent for a moment and then said, "It's to be a closed casket, Gabe, but the funeral people will open it for members of the family. Vonnie says Michael wanted it that way. You'll be able to see him one last time." Another silence and then, "Life's one big regret, isn't it?"

"Say hello to Kevin for me. I'll see you Monday." They hung up.

Sitting on the bed, Gabriel felt weak with weariness. He looked at Thea who was watching him from across the room. She said, "Come, let's have a steak and a bottle of wine."

In bed that night Gabriel couldn't sleep though he'd drunk three glasses of wine—the most alcohol he'd downed since he'd begun to taper off the booze. It hadn't helped him find sleep, however. Thea, as usual, slept deeply at his side. But Gabriel's head swarmed with images of Michael, Woodstock, and the waterfall.

He imagined Michael in a box in Missouri, the lid pressed on his face. He pictured his brother's life as a journey from Woodstock to West Plains, with a hundred stops in between, a passage of twenty thousand days. He thought, *What tricky paths we all travel to end in the earth though the real self has gone from the earth. My brother has gone from this earth.*

What did that really mean? Gone from earth. He couldn't get his mind around it. A voice sounded in his head: *But why should you expect to? Nobody else ever has either.*

Gabriel recognized the voice of Toby Myers. Did Toby, resurrected from dreams of childhood, intend to plague him now as a presence in his adult skull?

Gabriel addressed Toby in audible words, but in a whisper, lest he wake Thea. "What do you want with me, Toby?"

To help you do the necessary.

Recalling the words of the lizard, Gabriel said, "What is it, this necessary?"

Are you pretending you don't know, pal?

"Go away, Toby. I'm sick of ghosts. I won't listen to you anymore." Willing himself to sleep, he closed his eyes.

Toby said, *Yeah, you get some rest, pal. I'll watch over you just like I used to.*

The next day, Sunday, the day before Gabriel was to fly to the funeral, drifted past without incident. He wrote in his journal: "Come on, God. If you exist, be a sport. Show yourself in some form I'll recognize. You have three days to come through, you old fraud."

He started to put the book aside but hesitated. Should he note the latest quirk in his psyche, the rebirth of Toby Myers? Why not? It was part of the record. He wrote on.

> I seem to have brought Toby Myers to life again, not just as a dream memory of my boyhood but as a contemporary, a companion ghost in the here and now. In his heyday as my secret pal, Toby was not only visible to me, but we also talked aloud to each other. Now he's come back as a voice in my head, and invisible. But he's definitely here again. I should have anticipated as much. After all it was surely Toby who taunted me with that refrain: *You wasted your life. Like a piss in the ocean.* Maybe if matters go on in this vein long enough, instead of an interior voice, I'll dredge up a full-blown Toby, visible and articulate just like the old days. Right now, though, it seems to me I just have to hang on and take what comes. Hang, Gabriel, hang.

Later that day Gabriel tried to read the *Times,* but he couldn't focus his mind on the page. He kept imagining what might await him in the Ozarks. Would Michael's family treat him with hostility? Would Beth try to analyze him? Would he encounter Michael's ghost as he had Toby Myers?

As the day at last faded toward twilight, Valerie came to him. "I'm going to have a drink, Dad. Want one?" He shook his head. Apparently the closer to insanity he skated, the less he desired alcohol.

Later, in the study, he wrote a note to Richard: "When you were leaving the other day, you said that you love me. But I didn't get a chance to tell you the same because Benji interrupted. But I want you to know this, Richard: I love you too, and I think I sense the struggle within you. If ever you need me for anything, just say so. Dad."

Still later, in bed, Thea already into her profound sleep, his bag already packed for his journey the next day, Gabriel's mind hustled from point to point, reminding him of the spider he'd observed on the ceiling yesterday morning. What if nothing came of all this turmoil? What if the waterfall turned out to be just water? And if his offer to God went unanswered, what did it prove? Maybe only that he was crazy. Like Joyce.

CHAPTER 11

YOUNG GABE IS WATCHING a comedy starring a silent-film actor named Harold Lloyd. He is twelve, and alone in this nearly empty movie house called the Laff-Movie on Times Square. Harold Lloyd, in clerkly glasses, is clinging to a flagpole high over an avenue seething with traffic. Everything is in black and white. The flagpole, with no flag attached, juts out horizontally from the building. Harold Lloyd hangs on with his hands and feet wrapped around the pole. He is squirming in a frenzy of fear. Far below, so far below that if he fell Harold Lloyd would end up as a blot on the sidewalk, the cars and buses honk along the pavement. Harold Lloyd thrashes in terror. Young Gabe tells himself, *This isn't funny. This is scary. I don't want to look at this. I want to close my eyes.* But he can't take his eyes from the screen. He feels a heavy hand between his legs. Without turning his head, he looks to his right, and by the light from the screen, he sees the owner of the hand huddled in the seat beside him.

The man is bald and fat. He is breathing hard, mouth open as if he has just run a long distance. The man's breath smells of popcorn. The man keeps his eyes on the screen as his hand touches young Gabe. But then Toby Myers comes to take young Gabe's place with the man. Safe now, with Toby in his skin, young Gabe can watch without taking part.

In the light that jumps from the screen, Toby notices the sweat on the bald man's skull. And he notices the man's collar. The man is a priest. Toby speaks a familiar phrase: "Bless me, Father, for I have sinned." It is

Camel sign, Times Square—yes, it had all happened like that. Another lake of shit dredged from the depths of memory. Suddenly Toby's voice sounded in his head: *Put all that aside. Michael is dead in Missouri. Little Michael gone from this earth.*

Thea said, "Val wants to stay over a couple of extra days, to be here when you get back from the funeral. Is that all right with you?"

"Sure."

Had that man really been a priest? Toby said, *Yes, Stupid, yes.*

Gabriel finished the toast and drank a glass of grapefruit juice. Keep focused on the immediate.

"Plenty of gas in the Jeep?" Thea nodded and started putting the dishes in the washer.

Telling her he'd meet her outside, Gabriel picked up his bag, Italian leather purchased in Florence, and went out into the darkness before dawn. Lest he soak his only good pair of shoes in the dew, he avoided the grass by making his way along the gravel path to the edge of the stream. He stood in the blackness and listened to the pounding of the falls, still invisible in the night. He definitely heard garbled words in that rushing water. He minded a question to the unseen waters: *What are you saying?*

Far off the first birds of the morning began announcing themselves. Moments later the Jeep backed out of the garage. He walked away from the falls to join Thea.

She drove in silence along deserted Route 28. They were heading toward the Thruway. Then they would turn south to Newburgh and the airport.

After a while Gabriel said, "Do you really want to go live with Richard and Joyce, Thea?"

"Let's not talk about that now."

They eased onto the Thruway just as the first rose of dawn showed itself. The Jeep flew past the semis and milk trucks making their way to the city ninety miles away.

Thea said, "This is good for you, Gabe, this trip. It'll purge you of all the crap you still carry around inside you. It'll change you. I feel it."

The dawn bloomed into a glorious summer morning. Gabriel recalled the sound of the waterfall as he'd heard it earlier in the darkness. The memory provoked him to put a question to Thea. He had not yet spoken to her of the waterfall, but now it seemed right to make some effort, however oblique, in that direction. "Thea, when you go out by the waterfall, do you ever hear anything that sounds like words?"

She looked away from the road long enough to shoot a glance of puzzlement at him. He tried to explain. "You know. When the water splatters down, it makes that whooshing sound. Over and over, the same rhythm. Sometimes it sounds like words to me."

"What words?"

"That's just it, I can't make them out."

"I've never heard words. But I know what you mean about the rhythm. It can hypnotize you. You can stand there feeling spellbound. Maybe that's what you hear, that hypnotic rushing."

"Yeah."

They entered the airport grounds.

The sun cast long early shadows. Thea parked the Jeep at the curb under the indifferent eyes of a yawning security guard. Beyond a cyclone fence Gabriel spotted a Beechcraft commuter plane on the tarmac—no doubt the one he would soon have to board for the first leg of the journey.

Gabriel and Thea both got out of the car, Gabriel with bag in hand. They kissed. He held her close against him. "I love you."

"Something good is happening, Gabe. I know it. Let it happen. Please."

"I'll see you tomorrow night."

They kissed again. He walked away toward the plane. Something good is happening, she'd said. He hoped so.

As he ducked into the Beechcraft's cabin, he heard Toby Myers: *I'm coming with you.* Gabriel wasn't surprised. Weren't they reforging the bonds of old?

The plane from St. Louis landed in Springfield just before noon. Carrying his bag, Gabriel found his way to the frigidly air-conditioned terminal where he was to meet someone named Phyllis Tate who would drive him on to West Plains. He reminded himself to avoid anticipation of what lay ahead. For the next few hours he had to concentrate on the moment and accept whatever came his way.

Glancing about the waiting area, Gabriel spotted a tall young woman who was smiling and waving in his direction. He acknowledged her wave.

As he approached her, he saw that she was strikingly beautiful: dark hair to her shoulders, olive skin browned from the sun, classically sculptured face, light eyes, bright smile—a stunner. She was also about six feet tall and certainly no more than thirty. She wore a black dress that reached almost to her ankles. Her slim arms were bare. A blondish young man accompanied her. Shorter than she, he wore knee-length shorts, a white T-shirt, and running shoes. Gabriel felt himself grinning like an adolescent in the presence of the lovely young woman.

"Phyllis?" he said.

The beauty trilled a laugh. "Phyllis couldn't make it. I'm Mona."

She stuck out her hand. Gabriel clasped it. This towering Mona, he realized with a start, was his niece, Michael's daughter by his first wife. Gabriel remembered Mona's mother, Olivia, whom he had met only twice and who had died fifteen years ago, as a rather ordinary pretty girl. But the woman opposite was ravishing. Perhaps an influx of her father's Fallon genes had ratcheted up her mother's commonplace prettiness to produce the radiant Mona. And yet, except for her straight nose, there seemed to be little of the Fallon strain in her face.

Retrieving her hand, Mona said, "This is my husband, Daniel."

Gabriel shook the hand of the blondish young man.

Mona said, "We've been delegated to meet you and drive you to West Plains, Uncle Gabe."

Uncle Gabe. He'd have to get used to the appellation. Here in Missouri he would be Uncle Gabe until he left for home again.

Mona said, "Shall we get going?" Gabriel detected just a trace of a mid-America accent in her voice. He found it charming.

They went out into a blast of light and heat. They found the car—a white Cavalier that looked to Gabriel like vanilla ice cream melting in the noonday sun.

Daniel slid behind the wheel. Mona motioned for Gabriel to take the backseat. "You're so tall, you'll need the room." He clambered in with his Florentine bag. Mona took her place next to her husband. They drove off.

They passed, without conversation, through a district of billboards, motels, and fast-food restaurants. Only when the car reached a countryside of grassy hills and tree-lined pastures where herds of cattle grazed did Mona break the silence.

Twisting around toward Gabriel, she said that the family, as well as Michael's friends, were now gathering near the funeral home for a luncheon and reminiscing, as she put it, prior to the four o'clock church service. She suggested that, since it was just noon, Gabriel had ample time to check into his motel and settle in before going on to the funeral home. Gabriel agreed. He would like to clean up, call Thea, and take a breath before encountering Michael's two sons—especially if they proved as formidable as Mona.

Mona shot him one of her smiles. "It's settled then. We'll drop you off at your motel and pick you up a half hour later."

As they sped on, Gabriel noticed columns of smoke rising into the still air. Daniel said, "That's ranchers burning off brush."

Mona spoke again, this time not turning to Gabriel. "It's a closed casket, you know."

"I was told."

"But Vonnie's arranged for you to view the body, if you want to of course."

"Yes, I do want to."

Traffic on the highway seemed to consist mostly of pickups and trailer trucks—and few of those. From time to time a car would race past in defiance of the speed limit. Mona continued to talk. She spoke of her brothers, their careers, and her relationship with her father. "Daddy could be difficult. He had a temper. He could be strict. Sometimes he could even be harsh. But he meant well and I loved him very much. All of us loved him."

Gabriel said nothing, but he thought, *Little Michael, a patriarch, the father of this beautiful woman and her brothers.*

Mona talked of her own two children. "Wild imps sometimes. Six and four. Boys, of course. I'd like a girl." She talked of Vonnie. "I was surprised when Daddy married her. She was so different from my mother."

Gabriel said, "How so?" He thought he already knew the answer: Olivia had been pretty and educated; Yvonne was neither. But he wanted to hear Mona's view of her stepmother.

To answer Gabriel's query, Mona turned to look at him again. "My mother was lovely but not exactly forceful. Vonnie is just the opposite."

Gabriel ventured to agree with his niece's assessment, though he hardly knew Vonnie. Still twisted about, looking at him, Mona veered onto another topic, one that caught Gabriel off guard. "You know that Daddy used to drink?"

"I heard something about it."

"Well, it's no secret. He always had something of a problem, even when my mother was alive. But when she died, it got a lot worse. Then Vonnie came along and cured him. Or anyway she helped him to get better. My brothers and I will always be grateful for that. Daddy wasn't very nice when he was drinking." A shadow of sadness clouded her face, as if she was remembering some unhappiness involving her father. In the silence Gabriel could hear the hum of the engine and the hissing of the tires on the pavement. Then the bad moment receded. Mona's smile returned. "What do you think of our Ozarks countryside, Uncle Gabe?"

"Very pretty."

She chattered on, flitting from one subject to another without a pause. Gabriel found himself admiring what seemed to him her extraordinary ability to mask her grief in this way. He thought it probable that—like Vonnie—she was operating on nervous energy, had put off grieving until a later time. And perhaps she also felt unsure about how to treat her Uncle Gabe, the stranger she'd never met but only heard about—and who knew in what context? And so she talked.

As the car rolled into West Plains along Highway 63, it seemed to Gabriel that the town, or what he could see of it from the road, consisted of mall stores and highway outlets: Meek's Lumber, Taco Bell, and Wal-Mart.

Mona and Daniel dropped him off at the Best Western Motel. Promising to pick him up again in half an hour, they drove off.

Gabriel registered and went to room 211. The room was plain but clean and the air-conditioner worked. He set it at full-blast, washed his face, unpacked, and stretching on the bed, called Thea in Margaretville. She answered at once.

"Did the flight go all right?"

"Fine. I haven't been to the funeral home yet. Be going in a few minutes."

He told her about Mona, told her he missed her, and told her about the Ozarks' heat. Then he heard a knock on the door. He agreed to call again as soon he could after the funeral, no matter how late. He hung up to answer the door.

Mona, dressed as before but alone now, stood before him. Daniel, she explained, had some calls to make. She was going to take him to the funeral home herself.

As they drove away from the motel into a district of residential streets, Mona again began to chatter, most of it now a recital of her own career. She said that she held a master's degree in health education, whatever that meant, and despite having two small children to care for, she worked full-time as assistant athletic director for a college in Oklahoma whose name Gabriel didn't recognize. The job called for her to oversee the fitness and nutrition of the school's athletes. In addition to her work in Oklahoma, she served as a consultant in her field to high schools and professional sports teams. "Including the Kansas City Royals," she said with pride. Gabriel found it all impressive, especially for one so young, and he said so.

At a red light Mona turned to him with one of her luminous smiles. "My goal is to become the first woman athletic director of a major university."

"I admire your ambition."

"Daddy taught us well. 'Try or die,' he used to say."

That didn't sound like the Michael that Gabriel had known, the Michael who tended to give up when the going got rough. But then that memory came from decades ago. No doubt Michael, learning from experience and taught by life, had toughened up over the years. Gabriel asked Mona how she had gotten started in her field.

"Actually I got interested in fitness and nutrition when I was a model. I learned I had to take care of my body."

She went on to explain that as a teenager she'd had a stint as a fashion model for the Elite Agency in New York and spent two years working in Paris, Milan, and London. "But I discovered that I wanted a real life. So I decided to grow up and come home."

"To practice health and fitness."

"And to have babies."

Again his admiration welled up. He thought her a rare creature indeed—a beauty with a grip on reality.

Chapter 12

T HE FUNERAL HOME WAS a white-pillared, redbrick building with a blacktop parking area in the back. As Mona eased the Cavalier into a spot, Gabriel noted at least a score of cars already in the lot. Friends and family. He steeled himself for what lay ahead.

Mona, her face now a mask of solemnity, led him up concrete steps, through a glass door, and into a room with cream-colored walls and a burgundy carpet. A round cherry-wood table occupied the center of the room. There were no other furnishings. The air-conditioning made it seem cold after the heat of the parking lot. Despite the air-conditioning, the scent of flowers thickened the atmosphere.

Mona and Gabriel paused at the table as if to await someone in authority. A red velvet drape parted. A woman wearing a short-sleeved black dress and horn-rimmed glasses entered. It took Gabriel a moment to recognize Yvonne. His mind flashed back to the dinner with her and Michael six years earlier. She seemed unchanged, still gaunt of face and body. With her narrow eyes, hollow cheeks, down-turned mouth, and graying hair, she reminded Gabriel, as she had at their previous encounter, of a worn farm wife. In comparison with Mona, who towered over her like a willow over a thorn bush, she seemed lifeless, as if the stress of Michael's dying had drained her of most of her vitality.

In her smoker's voice, Yvonne said, "Gabe."

Feeling awkward, he embraced her. The bones of her shoulders moved under his palms. He muttered some phrase of sympathy.

She stepped back out of his embrace. "I'm glad you came. Thank you."

Instead of responding, he cleared his throat. Why did she consider it necessary to thank him for coming to his brother's funeral? Did she suppose he might have ignored this leave-taking?

She said, "We're having a lunch. You must be hungry after your long trip. Would you like something to eat?"

It came to him that she handled her pain this way, by clinging to the practical, making arrangements, seeing to things. How snobbishly he'd treated her in the past! Declining her invitation to eat, he asked for water.

Mona said, "I'll fetch it." She had been watching Yvonne with interest, as if assessing the performance of her father's plain but capable second wife, so different from her own pretty but ineffectual mother.

As Mona went off to fetch his water, Gabriel said to Yvonne, "She's lovely."

"Yes. Michael was very proud of Mona. But he was proud of all his children. He was a man of family, you know. His neighbors respected him, liked him. He had a lot of friends. Most of them are here today. Mikey would have liked that." She smiled as if the sentiment embarrassed her. "Sorry. Sometimes these days I find myself going on like that, honking like an old goose about nothing."

Mona returned with a tumbler of water. Gabriel drank it off and handed the glass back to her. She placed a tissue on the table and set the glass on it. Then she said to Yvonne, "I have to go pick up Daniel and the boys for the funeral." She bestowed one of her radiant smiles on Gabriel. "I'll see you later, Uncle Gabe." Intent on her errand, she went back into the heat of the day.

Yvonne led Gabriel through the red drape and down a hallway. They entered a room that looked like some kind of hall attached to the funeral home. Daylight poured through a row of windows high up on a wall. Fifty or sixty people, children as well as adults, everyone dressed in their Sunday best, sat at tables laden with sandwiches, pastries, and pitchers of iced tea. Gabriel surmised that most of these people were the neighbors and friends that Yvonne had mentioned earlier—gathered here for the funeral to come. He followed in Yvonne's wake as she advanced through the throng, greeting this one or that one, and introducing Gabriel as she passed. "This is Mike's brother, Gabriel, from New York." Smiling, Gabriel mumbled thanks for the condolences he heard on every side.

He spied Beth seated with a man in the back of the room. Beth and her companion, alone at their table, seemed deep in conversation. Beth hadn't yet sighted Gabriel. Excusing himself to Yvonne, he began to make his way toward Beth. As he did so, it dawned on him that the man at his sister's side was probably their cousin Kevin.

Gabriel noted that Beth still looked much as she had two years earlier when he and Thea had met her in Seattle for a drink. She had trimmed her hair a trifle shorter perhaps and more strands of gray salted the black, but otherwise she seemed the same stocky Beth with her Fallon nose, chin, and smile. Today she wore black, a dress much like Mona's.

Arriving at her table, strewn with sandwiches and pitchers of iced tea and surrounded by unoccupied folding chairs, Gabriel said, "Hello, Beth."

She looked up and broke into a grin of welcome. "Gabe! You made it! We thought you missed a plane. We were about to give up on you." She fingered the neck of her dress where, Gabriel recalled, she usually wore a string of pearls, absent on this day of mourning but fingered in absentia, out of habit. "Sit down, Gabe. Sit down."

Unlike Yvonne, Beth made no move to embrace him. He hadn't expected her to do so. It was not her way. Still he knew she was glad to see him. Though Beth and he seldom met, when they did they got along well. Sometimes her interest in psychology impelled her to overanalyze matters better left alone, but he liked her. He found her intelligent, articulate, well-traveled, and good-humored—though sometimes acerbic. He eased himself down on one of the folding chairs across from her and the man who had to be Cousin Kevin.

Beth said, "It seems odd that I have to introduce you two, but Gabe, this is Kevin, my faithful companion since I arrived in West Plains three days ago."

Kevin and Gabriel nodded at each other, each sensing that a handshake, as between strangers, would be somehow inappropriate. Kevin said, "It's good to see you, Gabriel. Too bad it has to be on such an occasion."

Gabriel mumbled a reply. Kevin set to fixing himself a glass of iced tea. As he did so, Gabriel noted that he was about six feet tall and almost, but not quite, fat. Stout might describe him. If memory served, Kevin was fifty-six or seven, although he seemed older to Gabriel. He wore his once-dark hair, now graying and receding, close-cropped in Prussian-officer style. His face, brown from years of exposure to the Texas sun and spotted with moles, sported a gray mustache that curled over his upper lip. A pair of bifocals sat on his nose. He had dressed in a dark suit, white shirt, and plain navy tie—all top of the line. Black Italian loafers shone on his feet and a Rolex glittered on his left wrist. Clearly Kevin did not shrink from proclaiming his opulence.

Gabriel also recognized that, despite the fleshiness that came close to disguising them, the Fallon features could still show in Kevin's face: the square jaw, the wide brow, the hooded eyes, even the nose, though in Kevin's case tiny broken veins marred the nose. And yet, this cousin bore little resemblance to either Beth or Gabriel. It was as if in Kevin the Fallon genes had assembled themselves to yield a being that was, and at the same time was not, familiar.

Gabriel hadn't encountered this cousin of his since their teen years. At that time Kevin, the oldest of the Fallon cousins, had earned repute as both a scholar and an athlete at Brooklyn Prep, the Jesuit secondary school that all young Fallons, except Gabriel, attended. Because their parents too often praised Kevin's achievements in contrast to the shortcomings of their own offspring, the teenage Fallons of the time had detested their older cousin. But Gabriel had not shared in the antipathy. As a student at Fordham Prep in the Bronx, where he too had excelled in both studies and athletics, he had escaped the shadow of Kevin. Thus he had not learned to loathe the paragon. In fact as a teenager he had hardly known his cousin and had heard only bits and pieces about him in the nearly forty years since then. Gabriel knew that Kevin had a doctorate in geology, held patents having to do with oil-drilling equipment, had married, and had children. But all this he had gleaned only second hand. Now, seated at the luncheon table prior to his brother's funeral, Gabriel listened as Kevin proceeded to recite for him, in detail, a recapitulation of his life.

Gabriel heard that his cousin's current marriage (his second) to Florence was a happy one and had lasted for more than two decades. He also gathered that Kevin lived in Dallas, was the chief of research for an oil company, and intended to retire soon to his ranch in Colorado where he planned to ski and raise horses with Florence. He had two grown children, girls, both of whom Kevin implied were as brilliant and successful as their father, though they had disavowed their Catholic heritage—a circumstance that pained him greatly. He still loved them, however, even though they had so far failed to provide him with grandchildren. His second marriage—"Don't ask about the first!"—was the anchor of his existence. He was a happy man—"Or anyway content!"—and he had become fond of Gabriel's brother, Michael, after they had encountered each other at a business conference a year ago.

"Michael was the kind of guy who couldn't do enough for you, if he liked you," Kevin said. "And I'm that kind of guy too. No jealousy in Michael. He was just good people." Gabriel could only nod in agreement.

Kevin continued his monologue, speaking about a book he intended to write, his travels in Europe, and a seminar course in geology he had recently given at Berkeley. He didn't ask anything about Gabriel, and Gabriel volunteered nothing. Instead he listened in silence, conceding Kevin's intelligence and eloquence but finding him increasingly tedious. As Kevin ground on, Gabriel noted a sardonic half smile on Beth's face. He reckoned that for the past three days she had served as the target of Kevin's garrulous self-absorption. Now it amused her to observe Gabriel caught in their cousin's line of fire.

Gabriel had begun to wonder how long Kevin could go on with his soliloquy, when Yvonne appeared. "Would you like to view the body, Gabe?"

"Yes."

Beth said, "I'll go with you."

Kevin, to Gabriel's relief, made no move to accompany them.

Yvonne led Beth and Gabriel away from the luncheon, back to the funeral home, down a corridor, and into a hushed room that felt almost chilly from the air-conditioning. Here on a gurney reposed a closed coffin of polished wood. Alone in the chamber, Beth, Yvonne, and Gabriel halted about ten feet away from it. The lid of the casket gleamed. A bald man, whom Yvonne identified as the funeral director, entered and began to unfasten the coffin's top.

Beth whispered, "Prepare for a shock. He looks like a mummy in there."

The funeral director lifted the lid and gestured permission to view the remains of Michael Fallon. Gabriel took a breath and gazed into the white-satin-lined box.

Michael lay flat in the pose of the dead: eyes shut behind horn-rimmed glasses and bony hands crossed on his abdomen. Gabriel noted bruises on the hands. He supposed that the administration of morphine had caused these blotches. Michael's face, sharp as a hatchet, was still a Fallon face but transformed to a bloodless mask—eyelids, cheeks, and brows like chalk. Where had Michael's freckles gone? Had suffering erased them? Or had the embalmer done it? His hair, wholly white and thin enough to show patches of scalp, looked like false stuff pasted to the skull. He wore a gray suit, white shirt, and dark tie—or at least the top half of him did, for only his upper body was visible in the coffin. The jacket and shirt were too big for his shrunken form, causing his neck and wrists to stick out like sticks. The jacket had no shape to it, as if no flesh lay under the folds, as if the cloth contained only dust and bones. Gabriel gazed down and thought, *My brother, gone from the earth.* He heard Toby Myers say, *Our brother gone from the earth.*

Gabriel thought of Michael as a boy with his shock of dark-brown hair and the scattering of freckles on his face, and he heard her voice also sound in his mind: *Take care of Michael.* But Gabriel hadn't taken care of him. He'd run away from him. Toby said, *Yes, you ran away from him.*

As Gabriel stood by the casket, eyes fixed on Michael still as ice, images came swimming up from wherever they lay hidden. He saw Michael trailing after him as they crossed a frozen Woodstock pond. He saw Michael leaping from a rock pile into a flooded stone quarry on the Keller property. Unable to swim, freckle-faced Michael had trusted his elder brother to keep him afloat once he surfaced again in the soupy water. He saw Michael petting a dog, Jake's Labrador retriever, Adolph. As these memories swam up, Gabriel thought, *This was my brother.* Tears clouded his eyes. This was what life came down to: dust in a box of white satin. Toby said, *Dust and regret too.*

Gabriel couldn't get past the regret that he had run from Michael and from the past that Michael represented. And despite the running away, Gabriel knew that he had escaped nothing after all. The past had never died. Exhumed like Toby Myers, it clamped him and Michael together—two men, one now beyond regret, who would remain linked to the boys they once were and to each other, until the survivor too passed beyond regret. Tears fell onto Gabriel's cheeks. Beth said nothing, but Gabriel saw that she was watching him. Did it surprise her that he wept? He didn't care. He wept and didn't try to hide it.

He felt Yvonne's hand on his shoulder. He heard her murmur something that sounded like, "Brothers need each other." He replied through tears. "I was a bad brother." Toby said, *Yeah, you were. A lousy brother, pal.*

As they walked out, Gabriel stopped at the door and looked back. The undertaker was closing the box, shutting Michael in forever. No one would ever look on him again. His tears drying, Gabriel followed Beth and Yvonne back into the hall where Kevin, family, and friends waited. He kept thinking, *Gone from this earth.*

Seated once more at the table, across from Beth and Kevin, Gabriel again found himself accepting expressions of sympathy from neighbors and friends of Michael. They came to him one after another with memories of his brother. He listened, shook hands, mumbled, and kept a smile on his face. His cheeks soon ached from the effort. Two figures in dark suits materialized on the other side of the table—Michael's sons. Gabriel rose, reached across, and shook hands with both of them. Evincing no resentment of their stranger-uncle, they drew up chairs and sat. As Beth and the ever-loquacious Kevin engaged them in conversation, Gabriel took the opportunity to assess these nephews he had never met.

Lawrence, the elder of the two, the doctor from New Orleans, was a handsome young man of perhaps twenty-eight. Tall, almost Gabriel's height, he had the pale look of one who spends most of his time indoors—a physician's hospital pallor no doubt. A thicket of brown curls much like Michael's in early manhood crowned Lawrence's Fallonesque face. He seemed at ease as he sat with his shoulders hunched forward and his hands folded on the table before him. He spoke in a straightforward manner, his voice low, his smile quick, his blue eyes aimed at his listener. Clearly, Lawrence, articulate and intelligent, knew who he was and where he was going. Gabriel liked him.

Peter, the younger brother, resembled his sister, Mona, more than his brother. He had Mona's dark good looks and sleek black hair—which he flaunted in a ponytail. He was twenty-three. He had just achieved his master's degree in education at Texas University. Like Mona, Peter was a smiler. He also seemed more than a little show-offy. Gabriel liked him well enough, though he suspected that, unlike Lawrence, Peter might prove tiresome with exposure. Just now Peter was describing his father's conservative proclivities as a disciplinarian.

"Dad favored the strap. It was his weapon of choice, especially when he was in his cups. But then with puberty—ours not his—he abandoned the leather and took to bribing us with money, a much more effective arrangement." When his audience reacted without enthusiasm to his essay at wit, Peter hastened to add a statement of affection for his father that seemed more natural to him than mannered cleverness. "Everybody loved my father. No better man ever lived."

A moment of solemnity followed. Then, under Kevin's prodding, the conversation flitted on to an appreciation of Yvonne's stoicism and memories of Michael as civic leader, softball player, scoutmaster, and Rotarian. Gabriel noticed no signs of grief in Lawrence or Peter, no trembling speech or red-rimmed eyes. He surmised that, like Yvonne, they did their mourning in private. At one point Lawrence said, "Dad was always a participant in the community, and yet he was a perennial outsider. They never really accepted him here."

Gabriel said, "Still it looks like he had lots of friends."

"Dad was liked. Not accepted. He was a happy man though. Certainly he had a happy life with Yvonne."

Did Lawrence mean to imply that Michael had had a less happy life with Olivia? But what did it matter now that Michael lay in a box that no one would ever open again?

The talk went on. Like Kevin, neither Lawrence nor Peter displayed any interest in learning about Gabriel. Although he found their lack of curiosity odd, he dismissed it and volunteered no information of his own. He hadn't come to West Plains to talk about himself.

All at once the funeral director, who had unsealed Michael's coffin earlier, appeared in the throng. He announced that the cortege would soon depart for the church and Michael's funeral. Explaining that they had some arrangements to see to, Lawrence and Peter rose and excused themselves.

As they made their way out of the room, Kevin said, "That Peter's a little hard to take." Beth smiled. "Hey, he's twenty-three. Cut him some slack."

The funeral director's assistants now passed through the room. They handed out programs for the church service. Michael's obituary, printed on black-bordered white paper, accompanied the program. Gabriel read through the obit. It contained all the standard information: birth, family, survivors, career, local affiliations, clubs—a digest of what Michael himself had called an ordinary life. But one reference in the obit brought Gabriel up short: Mr. Fallon played varsity football for Notre Dame University in the early 1960s. False. Michael had never attended Notre Dame, nor had he ever possessed the athletic prowess to play big-time college football. Either the obit writer had gotten his facts wrong or—more likely—Michael had concocted this fiction for some reason and it had become part of his life's story, eventually ending up in his obituary.

Beth also noted the football reference. Pointing to the sentence in the obit, she said to Gabriel, "That isn't true, is it?"

"No, but I guess it's part of his myth now." She nodded, acknowledging that neither of them would challenge the obit.

The funeral director's men now escorted Beth, Kevin, and Gabriel out to the parking lot to take their places in the cortege. They found that Mona, Lawrence, and Peter would travel to the church in the funeral director's limousine, immediately behind the hearse. Beth, Kevin, and Gabriel would follow in a second car with Vonnie. It puzzled Gabriel that Vonnie, the widow, had no place in the limo with Michael's children. Did this separation signify some ill will between one or more of Michael's children and Vonnie?

Within minutes the procession of cars arrived at a white-painted church on a residential street. "Faith Lutheran" proclaimed the sign over the entrance. Michael, though born a Catholic, had been a desultory parishioner here.

The mourners followed the casket out of the glare and heat into the modest interior of the church with pews arranged on both sides of a center aisle, an altar behind a railing of wood, a lectern, and an organ. Streams of light flooded through two stained-glass windows depicting the Crucifixion and the Resurrection. Ushers directed Beth, Kevin, and Gabriel into the first pew on the left side of the church. The rest of the family, Vonnie now among them, occupied the first pew on the right. Fifty or so mourners crowded into the remaining seats. Another score had to stand in the back, under the glow of stained glass. The casket, decorated with a spray of lilies, lay on a gurney within the gate leading to the altar. Gabriel stared at it, imagining Michael shut inside. The organ played. The funeral began.

CHAPTER 13

P AYING SCANT ATTENTION TO the service, Gabriel continued to stare at the casket while images of Michael as a boy, as a teenager, as a young man, surged from his memory. He recollected a day, a hot summer day much like this day of Michael's funeral, when he and Michael were living with their parents in their grandfather's house. Gabriel was fourteen, Michael eleven. Beth was a baby. By now Gabriel's made-up companion Toby Myers had receded from his life. Thus he was no longer young Gabe, but Gabriel. Somehow, while goofing around in their grandfather's garden, Michael and Gabriel had gotten into a dispute whose cause Gabriel could not recall. It had begun as a scuffle, a wrestling match, but then—he could recall this part perfectly—Gabriel had erupted into fury. All the hurt of his young life had suddenly crystallized. All the anger he felt for his mother and father—usually suppressed—broke loose, and he hurled the full load at Michael. Roaring with rage, blind, choking, and cursing, Gabriel struck his brother with fists and feet. He threw Michael to the ground. He beat him on the face and skull. Grabbing him by the hair, Gabriel pounded Michael's head against the hard-packed earth until he lay motionless and bleeding. And still Gabriel howled and cursed. He would have gone on hitting Michael if his arms hadn't grown too weary to do so. Only when his horrified grandfather came and pulled him off the prostrate Michael did Gabriel perceive what he'd done. With no Toby to take the blame, he recognized that evil lived in him—and he'd broken down in sobs of remorse while Michael, bleeding from nose and mouth,

126

lay stunned, a victim of something mysterious that afflicted his wild, big brother, something beyond his understanding.

Gabriel also remembered what his grandfather kept muttering as he had clutched Gabriel in his arms: "What have they made of you boys? What have they done to you?" Later that night as Michael and Gabriel lay in their cots in the room they shared, Michael—bandaged and calm—had whispered in the dark, "It's okay, Gabe. I get mad sometimes too. It's okay." With his eyes fixed on the box that contained all that remained of Michael, Gabriel thought, *He could forgive me, but I couldn't forgive myself.* Suddenly he heard Toby: *You should have kept me around, pal. You needed me.*

As the minister droned on, another picture came into Gabriel's mind: a hospital scene a dozen years later. His father—their father, their selfish, neglectful, cruel father—lay dying of lung cancer. The disease had rendered him unable to talk, unable to boast, or to mock. Disdaining to act the hypocrite, Gabriel had paid only cursory visits to the hospital. But Michael, then in his twenties, spent hours at the mute man's sickbed. He also performed tasks that disgusted Gabriel: cutting the curled-up toenails, shaving the slack jaw, washing the festering genitals, brushing the foul teeth, all with a tenderness Gabriel found at once revolting and incomprehensible, a misplaced solicitude for the man who had wounded him and Michael—and distorted their lives without scruple.

Michael had protested Gabriel's lack of compassion. "He's our father, for Christ's sake!" But Gabriel had turned his back without regret. Michael, he'd told himself then, was a better man than he was, but Gabriel could not forgive—and would not pretend what he couldn't feel.

Standing now, in obedience to one of the ceremonial movements of the service, Gabriel reread Michael's obit. Notre Dame Varsity Football. An ordinary life. False and true. But the obit said nothing about Michael's drinking or about Vonnie's rescuing him from that pit. The obit also failed to note Michael's resolve to educate his children, his true achievement. Nothing in the obit told of his disappointments, his inner life, his failures and triumphs. What passions moved him? Had he soared with joy when he taught his classes at the college? What did he regret? The obit told none of that. But it trumpeted the fiction of Notre Dame football. Gabriel thought, *No life is ordinary, but every life is a mystery.*

He became aware that the church had fallen silent. The minister had finished. The congregation had uttered its prayers. A stocky woman rose near the organist. In a voice as pure as it was small she began to sing "Danny Boy."

The pipes, the pipes are calling.
From glen to glen and down the mountainside.

Gabriel's tears flowed, and so did Beth's, and so did those of the assembly as the melancholy of the music, wedded to words of grief, squeezed their hearts. Gabriel wept, not only because the melody touched him, but also because he knew what no other in that gathering could know: this was the song that Michael often sang to himself in the darkness, his boy-voice cracked, the words askew, when, as children alone and abandoned, he and young Gabe had gone to their beds among strangers. The singer rendered the second verse.

But when ye come, and all the flowers are dying.
If I am dead, as dead I may well be.
You'll come and find the place where I am lying.
And kneel and say an Ave there for me.

Gabriel heard not the singer but his boy brother singing in the dark in a bed near his own, airing some otherwise inexpressible emotion for both of them in his child's voice, among strangers. In the fearsome dark.

And I shall hear, though soft you tread above me.
And all my grave will warmer, sweeter be.

Gabriel knew that Michael himself had chosen this air to be sung here in this church on this day, because he knew that Gabriel would hear it and that Gabriel alone would grasp its meaning.

And I shall sleep in peace until you come to me.

And so Gabriel wept—for himself, the hearer of the song, as well as for the boy who once sang it, the boy in the box.

At the cemetery the mourners clustered beneath a blue-and-white striped canopy under which a grave lay open. Sheltering with the others in the shadow of this awning, Gabriel watched as pallbearers placed the casket on a trellis above the hole in the earth. At a signal from the minister, one of the funeral director's men switched on a tape player that began to give off bagpipes rendering "Amazing Grace." Gabriel supposed that Michael had also chosen this hymn for this moment. Except for a breeze ruffling the canopy, the keening of the pipes was the only sound.

The music died away. The minister recited, "Dust to dust, ashes to ashes." More tears. Beautiful Mona dabbed at her eyes, hidden under dark glasses, with a dainty white handkerchief. Yvonne, stoic in black, stood like an image of heartache at the grave.

The minister droned to the finish and closed his book. The music of the pipes returned and then leaked away. The coffin rested on its trellis, awaiting its lowering into the hole after the mourners dispersed. The men who would carry out that ultimate act would not mourn. They would want only to get the job done then go home for supper and a couple of beers. They would joke and talk of sports as they covered the box with yellow Missouri soil.

The services concluded, family and friends milled about as if reluctant to part from each other. Some, Yvonne among them, stood by the box for a last farewell. Gabriel stepped out from under the canopy. He longed to depart the cemetery now. He had no more farewells in him. He could feel the sweat running down his back.

A middle-aged woman with jowls like a deflated volleyball began telling him how much she had liked his brother. "Mike Fallon was a great guy. We used to have such fun singing Irish songs! Mike knew every Irish song there was. Get a little whisky in him, and the Irish came out. A great guy." Gabriel nodded and felt relief when she took her jowls elsewhere.

Kevin emerged from under the canopy. He embraced Gabriel and then kissed his cheek. Gabriel was grateful that for once Kevin didn't feel the need to say anything. The mourners returned to the cars and drove away from the cemetery, making for Michael and Vonnie's house, which Gabriel had never seen. There family and friends would convene again.

As the car turned into the driveway, Gabriel examined the place that had been Michael's home—with Yvonne and before that with Olivia—for thirty years. Small, two stories high, built of wood, with a pitched roof, brown siding, and white trim, it stood in a street of similar houses. All of them seemed well kept, with lawns and hedges separating one from another and with red oaks and walnut trees providing shade. A pickup truck stood in the driveway next door to Michael's house

Following Yvonne and Beth through the front door, Gabriel discovered that the house was even smaller than it looked from outside. The living room was scarcely large enough to contain a couch, love seat, easy chair, and television set. He could see an old-fashioned bathroom just off the living room, and beyond that a boxy bedroom. A big kitchen, bigger in any case than the living room, occupied much of the first floor. Here on a Formica-topped counter reposed an array of food and liquor. An uncarpeted staircase led from the living room to the second floor where, Gabriel supposed, he would find additional bedrooms. He did not climb the stairs to see. *The house*, he thought, *resembled Michael himself and Yvonne too: ordinary, a place for living not pride.*

People swarmed in all the rooms: Michael's children and their spouses; Mona's two young boys; three heavy women whom Vonnie identified as her daughters from her previous marriage; neighbors; some of Michael's business associates, and of course Beth and Kevin, as well as Gabriel himself.

Taken to the kitchen, he refused the offers of food and liquor that came at him from every side. He had no appetite, but he couldn't seem to get enough water. He gulped glass after glass as strangers introduced themselves and told anecdotes about "Mike," most of which Gabriel had already heard several times.

Eventually he managed to work his way out of the kitchen and into the living room. Beth made space for him beside her on the couch. Kevin— in shirtsleeves now—sprawled on the love seat at right angles to them. Yvonne, who had changed into a T-shirt, shorts, and sandals, occupied the easy chair. She was smoking a cigarette.

Moments later young Peter drifted in. Lawrence and his wife—a physician like her husband—joined them soon after. The new arrivals sat opposite Beth, Kevin, and Gabriel on folding chairs from the kitchen. Like Yvonne, they had changed into T-shirts and shorts. Mona, still in her mourning dress, her smile radiant once more, remained in the kitchen to play hostess.

The evening became a marathon of talk. Lawrence and Candace (a slight young woman with intelligent brown eyes, short dark hair, and grave features) recounted some of their experiences as interns at their New Orleans hospital. Peter and Lawrence both spoke of their father with affection. The conversation expanded to include travel incidents, politics, the sins of the news media, and even the attractions available in the Ozarks. "Caves," said Peter, all seriousness. "The caves are marvelous. Limestone caverns. Fascinating."

Whatever the subject, however, Kevin—whose intelligence and good will Gabriel conceded—somehow contrived to make himself the focus of the colloquy. Time after time he brought the talk back to what *he'd* seen, what *he* knew, what *he'd* accomplished.

Gabriel wouldn't call it bragging per se, nor did he doubt Kevin's veracity. Nevertheless his cousin's self-focus repelled him. He had long theorized that this tendency to preen and magnify infected most Fallons. He could remember uncles and aunts who had indulged in just such self-glorification even when—as in Kevin's case—they had nothing to gain from doing so. Even Michael had exhibited the trait when he claimed to have played football at Notre Dame. And Gabriel had to admit that in his youth, feeling himself unworthy of his own aspirations, he had sometimes invented triumphs in order to fill himself up with something of merit. Later, as he had achieved at least some of the esteem he craved, he had fought free of the need to dilate on himself. Thus, as Kevin babbled on, Gabriel wanted to call out, "Shut up, Kevin! No more! You don't have to do this! We see you!" But he held his tongue, aware that any such admonition would produce no effect on his cousin—a Fallon, after all.

As the evening ground on toward ten, Beth suggested to Gabriel that they excuse themselves and get a hamburger together. "I'd like to have some time to talk with you alone, if you're up to it."

Although Gabriel calculated that, allowing for the time change between New York and Missouri, he'd gone without sleep for more than twenty hours, he welcomed some time alone with Beth. He knew she planned to fly to Houston at dawn—with Kevin in his company plane—and then go on to Seattle from there. Gabriel's own flight home would take off later at 3:00 p.m., and Vonnie had already arranged his transportation to Springfield. Clearly if he and Beth meant to have their talk, they had to do it soon, while she still had the time and he still had the energy for it.

Together Beth and Gabriel said good night to all. Kevin gave Gabriel another hug. Gabriel made a date to meet Vonnie at his motel in the morning for brunch and a further farewell. Finally Beth and Gabriel managed to break away. Borrowing the Hyundai that once belonged to Michael, they drove into the humid night, Beth behind the wheel.

CHAPTER 14

J UST OFF THE HIGHWAY they located a Pizza Hut and went in. Finding they were the only customers, they served themselves from the salad bar, chose a booth, and took a seat on opposite sides of a beige Formica table. They picked at their salads in what seemed to Gabriel a self-conscious silence. Meanwhile the teenage waitresses and busboys began mopping the floor and putting away cutlery, clearly the nightly ritual at closing time. The boys and girls with their mops and flirtatious patter appeared in no hurry to get rid of their last customers.

Beth said, "So, Gabe, how are you feeling after all that today?"

How was he feeling? He missed Thea. He said, "I feel like a surviving twin. It's odd, but I'm only now beginning to understand how much Michael and I shared, how strongly linked we were even after all the years apart."

She nodded. "Do you feel guilty for surviving?"

"That's a psychology student's question."

"Sorry. Just a reflex. No jargon tonight, Gabe. Only revelation."

He pushed his salad away unfinished. "Revelation? Tell." He waited for her to speak. She took a deep breath. "You don't know it. But I'm a survivor too."

Gabriel had no wish to contradict her, but it seemed to him that he and Michael had shared sorrows that Beth could never comprehend: the pain of abandonment, the feeling of worthlessness, the rejection by parents who, locked in their own savagery, used their children for ends that neither they nor the children could explain.

In a voice that reminded Gabriel of a penitent's murmuring in a confession booth, Beth said, "Mommy and Daddy did their number on me too."

He thought, *She calls them Mommy and Daddy.* Gabriel refused to use those terms to describe them. To him Mommy was a term of endearment, as was Daddy. Thea was a mommy. He himself was a daddy. Thea and he had earned those designations from their children. Gabriel's parents—Beth's parents—had never qualified.

Beth said, "Do you remember when Daddy put me in St. Cecilia's?"

Gabriel remembered it well. He'd been nineteen then, an escapee as he thought of it, and living on his own in the city. Beth had been—what? Five? A mop-headed doll. His father and mother, in one of their periods of separation, had begun battling over money, support payments, custody of Beth—any excuse to gnaw at each other. One day his father had seized Beth and brought her, screaming and terrified, to an upscale Catholic boarding school in Westchester. The nuns had taken the child in when her father—charming Daddy—had declared that he wished to save his child from the atheistic, syphilitic witch, Mommy.

Yes, Gabriel remembered the episode. He also recalled thinking then that Beth would have a better life with the nuns of St. Cecilia than with either of them. But in truth he'd spared little thought for his baby sister at the time. He was taking night courses at NYU and working at the *News,* trying to become a writer.

Now seated across from him in a Pizza Hut booth in West Plains, Missouri, Beth began to recount how life had unfolded for her at St. Cecilia Academy. "I was there alone. These imposing strangers in their black and white habits were all around me. Daddy went away. I cried night after night. I lived in terror. Why was I there? Dumped and forgotten. Why? What had I done? I couldn't stop crying. And I couldn't eat. The nuns used to push food down my throat. I was always choking and vomiting, making them angry with me. I kept wondering: Why doesn't Mommy come for me? Or Daddy? Can you imagine how I felt, Gabe, practically a baby, suddenly deserted like that?"

He nodded. Yes, he could imagine it. Hadn't he lived it too?

She said, "After what seemed a long time, but was probably only a month or so, I settled down at St. Cecilia's. Kids are resilient. They get used to their wounds. Daddy would visit me on occasional weekends. I'd never know when he might show up, and so the nuns would dress me in my best and I'd wait and pray for him to come and collect me in that ugly maroon Cadillac he drove then. Usually he didn't show, and I'd go to bed crying. But sometimes he did show. And then we would roar off together in his car, me in a bonnet and my best clothes. He would always tell me that Mommy didn't love me, didn't want me, and that's why she never came to see me. He would talk like that until I cried—and then he would stop, satisfied with my tears, I guess. It was as though he thought he was hurting her by hurting me, by making me hate her. But really he was making me hate myself. Why didn't Mommy love me? What had I done that she never came to see me?" She glanced across the table. "Pretty fucked-up childhood, no?"

"Pretty fucked up, yes." Gabriel had never heard any of this before. He always believed Beth liked St. Cecilia's because it sheltered her from the battles that swirled about her.

Beth went on. "Very often Daddy was into one of his drinking bouts when he picked me up for one of those infrequent weekends. Then he'd take me to his hangouts. The nightclubs, the gambling joints, bars, whatever. I found myself in these smoke-filled haunts of his, at parties where he'd show off cute little *Lizzie*. That was my name then, remember? Not Elizabeth but little Lizzie, so smart and bright. Daddy would have me sing and dance for his friends, men and women both, who'd clap and grin at me, sipping their drinks, smoking their Marlboros and Salems. I always sang 'Peg O' My Heart.' That was his favorite. I must have made him look like a prince to these people, his friends. But sometimes I got tired and fell asleep. If it was a party, they'd usually let me sleep under the coats in a bedroom. But lots of times, when he was really hitting the bottle, Daddy'd put me in the car alone while he went about doing whatever it was he was doing:

gambling, playing around with his women. Well, you know how he was, Gabe. Nothing mattered, least of all me, when he was on the hunt. So there I'd be, sleeping in the backseat of his car. I can't remember how many times I woke up cold and shivering in the dark. He'd forgotten all about my being there, of course. So there I would be, not knowing where I was, locked in the car, trapped, crying, thirsty, having to pee, but too afraid to call out. Lots of times I just had to pee in my pants. Then I'd hunch down on the floor behind the front seat of the car and pray to God that he would come back, that I wouldn't be left there forever. Once in a while, instead of the car, he would leave me in a hotel room. That was better than the car. At least I could go to the bathroom. But even in the hotel rooms I was afraid, thinking he wouldn't come back and I'd have to stay in there forever. But the worst was if he was drunk, I mean *really* drunk, when he did come back for me. Then he would cry and say how sorry he was, what a terrible father he was. He'd slobber all over me and touch me, call me his pretty Lizzie, tell me how much he wanted me to be happy. And I would find myself feeling sorry for *him* even as I hated the way he was hugging me and spewing his alcoholic breath into my face."

Gabriel thought of the Laff-Movie, the priest with the scalp that glowed with sweat.

Beth said, "I never told anyone about those weekends. I was ashamed. Sometimes in my room at St. Cecilia's, I thought I might tell you someday. But I never could. First of all you weren't around that much, but second I was really angry at you for going away, forsaking me." Suddenly she smiled across the table. "Am I beginning to sound like a survivor, Gabe?"

He nodded.

She went on. "I started to get fat. Remember? Well, maybe you don't. You weren't there, were you? Anyway, from not being able to eat at all, I became a gorging machine at St. Cecilia. I ate anything and everything. I used to steal whole cakes and pies from the pantry. I could eat a whole box of chocolates in ten minutes. On one occasion they caught me in the kitchen, standing in my pajamas by the light of the open fridge, my mouth stuffed with mashed potatoes. Can you imagine? Cold mashed potatoes dribbling from my mouth over my chin. The nuns were furious, and disgusted too—I could see it in their faces. They punished me with a whipping on my bare legs. But nothing could stop my eating. The nuns would try to discipline me in a lot of different ways: the strap, of course, sending me to bed without my supper, having to spend whole days in the chapel. Nothing worked. I always contrived to get food, often from the other girls who seemed to derive some kind of weird pleasure from my eating. In any event, I ballooned. I went from little Lizzie to Blimpo by the time I was eight. And of course, as I got fat, Daddy lost interest in me. He ignored me for longer and longer periods. And when he did see me, he mocked me. You know what he started to call me?"

Gabriel shook his head.

"Porkbelly."

Yes, Gabriel could hear him saying that, could picture the sneer on his lips.

"Daddy stopped paying the tuition at St. Cecilia's. They kicked me out. I went back to Mommy. I was nine by then. Fat Liz."

Gabriel could recollect little of Beth at that time. Thea and he had married. Michael had also started living on his own, working days and attending St. John's at night, courting Olivia. Neither Gabriel nor Michael had paid much attention to their sister. In fact, on those occasions when Gabriel had encountered Beth, she struck him as a surly child who sucked on candy from morning to night.

He said, "Did you ever tell her how he treated you?"

"Her? Mommy? Jesus, no! What could I tell her that she would care about, or even hear? All she cared about was herself. She complained and cried and was helpless."

Yes, that described her as she had grown older. As her beauty faded, she had retreated to a state of self-absorbed irritation and infirmity.

Beth went on. "Mommy made me her servant, you know. No, of course you don't know. You were busy making a life with Thea and your kids. I was only ugly, stupid Lizzie being punished for being fat and unlovable by slaving for her ice-cold mommy."

Gabriel said nothing. He regretted that he'd hurt Beth by his absence when she needed him, but he couldn't have helped her in any case. He had learned from his own experience that kids had to heal their own wounds. He had fled to make himself whole. Beth, too, had had to cope by herself. The healing only worked that way.

Beth said, "By the time I was twelve, I was doing everything for Mommy. I did all the shopping. I cooked and cleaned and even paid the bills. She complained and complained. She said I was disgustingly fat. She said she was ashamed to be seen with me. She would tell me how wretched her life had been with Daddy, how alone she was. Sometimes her misery would overwhelm her. She'd fly into a rage. She'd slap me in the face. She'd cry out that she couldn't stand the sight of me. I took it because I deserved it. I was Porkbelly Liz, wasn't I?

"One day, when I was fifteen and truly desperate, I asked her if she loved me. She only laughed. I implored her to say that she loved me. She laughed and refused. She made me get on my knees. I did. 'Beg me,' she commanded. I obeyed. She laughed and called me ugly. It went on like that for hours, my begging her to say she loved me, her laughing and refusing. In the end I gave up and collapsed. That was the day I decided that, like you and Michael, I had to go away, fat and ugly as I was, and find some kind of life of my own. I took refuge in photography—the darkroom made me feel safe. The camera seemed to me a miraculous instrument, a way to arrest time. I found, to my amazement, that I was good at it, me, Porkbelly Liz. Eventually I fled to the West, alone. I was terrified at first. I hoped I could separate myself from the past by changing my name to Beth and pursuing a career. I managed. I grew. But I really couldn't shake off the past. I found myself more and more drawn to studying myself, which explains my interest in psychology, right? And here I am, telling you everything." She took a deep breath and smiled. "Well, Gabe? Do I qualify as a survivor?"

He reached across the table and took her hand. How many years had she been waiting to relate her tale to him? For the first time he felt the tug of the blood they shared. In a way, since Michael had departed the earth, she was now his twin. He saw tears pooling in her eyes. If she began to weep, he would sit beside her, comfort her. But the tears did not fall.

She said, "You know, in spite of everything, I loved them. I cried bitterly at Daddy's funeral. And when Mommy died, I grieved even more." She paused as if to reflect on her grief back then, and then went on. "A child needs to love. So I understand why I loved them. What I don't understand, never could understand, were Mommy and Daddy themselves. They were always an enigma."

Squeezing her hand in his, Gabriel thought, *Not to me.* He had come to view Beth's Mommy and Daddy as prodigies of selfishness, makers of misery. True, you couldn't explain how they became such monsters. And that would always remain a mystery. But you could recognize—had to recognize—that such creatures do exist in the world—and then let it go lest they bedevil all your days. But he said none of this to Beth. Like him, she would have to attain that liberation on her own.

Beth said, "It always used to puzzle me why Mommy and Daddy stayed together as they did for as long as they did. I used to ask myself why they didn't just divorce instead of staying locked in their horrid ballet. And I finally came up with a theory: theirs was an inverted love. They were two scorpions clamped together, stinging each other. Scorpion love."

He nodded. Her description seemed as plausible as any other.

She said, "Tell me, after all these years, do you hate them? Or have you forgiven them?"

"Neither. Really, I just want to forget them. Bury them once and for all, so to speak."

Beth said, "Maybe we can be friends, Gabe."

He thought how much he liked her. They lived three thousand miles apart and had come together today only because of their brother's death. But they shared blood, as well as similar, if not common, memories. Perhaps they could be friends.

One of the teen waitresses, Kelli according to the badge on her red uniform, approached to announce that the Pizza Hut was closing. Gabriel consulted his watch; it was after 2:00 a.m. He'd been awake, and under stress, for twenty-four hours.

Beth drove him back to the Best Western. Then, as if reluctant to depart even now, they talked some more in the car—this time about their lives now. Beth told of her career. Galleries in San Francisco and Los Angeles had started to show her work. She would soon have her degree in psychology, which she referred to as her avocation.

"But I still don't really understand anything, especially about myself." She divulged nothing of her intimate life, however. If she had loves or lovers, she didn't say, and Gabriel didn't press her.

In contrast to her reticence, he confided in her without restraint that he had given up writing; that he had written nothing close to what he'd once hoped to write; that he considered his life a failure; that he feared losing his grip on reality—messages in waterfalls, bargains with God, the resurrection of a childhood ghost, thoughts of suicide plaguing a man sick of life but afraid of death.

She listened to his disclosures but did not comment except for murmurs of sympathy from time to time. He saw that these matters, so mighty in his own life, struck her as much less so. He gained the impression that she regarded him as just another creature facing mortality—a man choking on the fact that he would never accomplish what he had set out to do.

That she could not grasp the cataclysm of his failure revealed to his mind the gulf that still lay between them. Yes, he liked her, and he thought it probable that, after this night, she liked him. Yes, they could now regard each other as survivors of similar trauma, but neither of them would ever really comprehend the person the other had become. They had met each other's true self too late for that. Gabriel kissed her cheek and climbed out of the car. She drove away. Fighting exhaustion, he went into his motel.

CHAPTER 15

DESPITE THE LATENESS OF the hour, he kept his promise to call Thea. She answered on the third ring. "I've been dozing, waiting by the phone. How was it out there?"

Gabriel began telling her but broke it off. "I'll save the details for when I see you." He asked about her day.

"Val and I stopped in to see Ilse and Andrus. They were wonderful as always."

He recalled Andrus's saying: You learn something new every day but you still die stupid. Had Michael died stupid? Yes, of course.

Thea went on, telling about Ilse's canning, but he paid scant attention to the meaning of her words. Instead he concentrated on the sound of her voice. Her calm and sweetness soothed him.

He said, "I'll be home tomorrow night. I love you."

He fell into bed. But in spite of the weariness that had seeped into his bones, he couldn't sleep. He kept hearing the voices of the day in his head, as clear as if they occupied the room with him. Kevin's droning on, Peter's attempts at cleverness, Beth's "I'm a survivor too" all echoed in his mind. *Danny Boy, the pipes, the pipes are calling.* And then the voice of Toby Myers joined in: *You wasted your life. Do the necessary.*

Gabriel recognized these as auditory hallucinations, the product of exhaustion. He'd encountered them before after marathons of wakefulness. Experience had taught him that only sleep would shoo them away. But clearly sleep would not come yet. He would have to endure the jumble of sounds until it did. The Kevin voice vexed him most—droning, incessant, irritating. And yet despite his blustering, Kevin was kind, intelligent, honest—a man worth knowing. Still, even now, when only a presence in Gabriel's head, he would drone on!

Suddenly a raw new noise thrust aside the hallucinatory voices in his brain. A roar. It grew louder. And again louder. With a shock Gabriel recognized a familiar rhythm: Eternity Falls, its booming so true the falls might have materialized in the room. Tumultuous, insistent, it flooded Gabriel's mind. And once more he detected in its thunder words just beyond perception. Maddening. Then, as if some unearthly hand had turned up the volume, the elusive sounds coalesced and emerged. Gabriel heard at last the cataract's cry: *Surrender to me, Gabe! Nothing really matters!* There came into his mind a memory of Toby Myers urging him to do the necessary. Was this command to surrender a revelation of the necessary? To surrender? To surrender what? His life? Because nothing meant anything anyway? Over and over the phrases repeated in his ear. There was no mistaking it: *Surrender to me, Gabe! Nothing really matters!* His arrhythmic heart began to leap. He had to struggle for breath. The volume rose to a shout: Nothing really matters!

Gabriel covered his ears with his hands, trying to shut out the bodiless voice. Now that he could finally hear it, it filled him with dread. He wanted to hear it no longer. *Stop it!* he screamed into his own mind. *Stop it!* As if in obedience to his command, the clamor of the torrent began to diminish. The exhortation faded away with it. Silence descended upon the room. Gabriel could hear his breathing, easier now.

He lay flat on his back on the bed. He stared up into the darkness. He had soaked the bed sheets with his sweat. *Surrender to me, Gabe! Nothing really matters.* Was this truly the message of Eternity Falls, recaptured and decoded at last because lack of sleep had stripped his mind of distractions? And if the message was a recollected reality, what was it supposed to convey? He shuddered. Then, incapable of resistance, he slid into the oblivion of sleep.

Gabriel woke with the sun streaming into the room. He rolled over in the bed and lay flat on his back. Instantly the waterfall's urging of the night before resounded in his mind: *Surrender to me, Gabe!* He experienced a resurgence of the fear it had induced in him. But now, with bars of morning light lying across the bed, the menace receded almost at once. Had he really deciphered the waterfall's message, or had he only hallucinated it last night as he had hallucinated "Danny Boy" and the buzzing of Kevin and Toby Myers? No, no, Toby belonged to some other order of being, a ghost resurgent. He mustn't confuse the two ideas. Moreover the waterfall message he'd heard last night might have nothing at all to do with Eternity Falls. Perhaps it had been only some fucked-up manifestation of grief for Michael, or an expression of sorrow for his own botched existence—his wasted life, as Toby put it, his piss in the ocean.

Surrender to me, Gabe. Nothing really matters. What could those words possibly signify? A communication from God after all? A demand for self-destruction? In the light of the new day, he saw only one way to authenticate them: he had to hear them again in Eternity Falls itself. Thus he resolved that when he returned home, he would go and stand by the torrent. If he heard the exhortation then, he would have to concede that something—the falls or some part of himself—meant him to perceive (and obey?) that summons to surrender. And if he did hear that incantation again, he would do what had to be done: the necessary. In the meantime, for the sake of his sanity, Gabriel must think no more about these matters until he returned to Margaretville. Best to focus on the day ahead. Accordingly he rose and showered, dressed, and checked out. Then he went to the coffee shop to meet Yvonne for the brunch they had scheduled the day before.

Wearing a tan shirtdress, Yvonne was already seated at a table when Gabriel arrived. He was pleased to see that Lawrence and Candace accompanied her. As Gabriel took a chair, Lawrence explained that he and Candace were driving back to New Orleans that afternoon and wanted to come to the motel with Vonnie to say a farewell to Uncle Gabe. He welcomed their presence. It would minimize any awkwardness that he and Vonnie might feel with each other. In any case Gabriel found Lawrence and Candace the most interesting of the young members of Michael's family. Peter struck him as too show-offy for his own good, and Mona's self-absorbed ambition could wear you out. In contrast, Lawrence and

Candace impressed Gabriel as solidly grounded in their own life. Despite their youth, they knew where they'd come from and where they were going. They were serious people, and Gabriel liked them both very much.

Over a burger, which he ate but scarcely tasted, he chatted with them and Vonnie. The talk touched on scuba diving, a passion that Gabriel shared with both Lawrence and Candace, and memories of Michael as a father from Lawrence and as a boy in Woodstock from Gabriel. They talked also of Candace's recent decision to specialize in cardiology. They talked of New Orleans, a city all of them loved.

At one point Vonnie volunteered that she might soon depart West Plains. "Now that Mikey's gone, I'm thinking I might want to find some place new. I have friends in Kansas City."

Lawrence, beside her at the table, took her hand in his and held it, a clear expression of his esteem for her. It seemed to Gabriel that Lawrence, far more than Mona or Peter, grasped the heroism of Vonnie's rescue of Michael from his demons. Mona, on the other hand, had displayed a distinct edginess toward Vonnie throughout the funeral ceremonies— as if she harbored some resentment toward the woman who had taken her mother's place. Stepmother syndrome? But it was none of Gabriel's business. Still, Mona intrigued him, and he remarked on her beauty and her unusual career as a fitness and athletic expert, as well as her travels in Europe and her modeling career. But his praise of Mona elicited only a tilt of the head from Vonnie and an exchange of glances between Lawrence and his wife.

Candace said, "Mona exaggerates."

Lawrence said, "Did Mona tell you that she's a consultant to the Kansas City Royals?"

Gabriel nodded. Had Mona contrived a Fallonesque series of falsehoods for him? His heart sank at the idea of that splendid young woman resorting to unreality to fill up her life.

Lawrence now elaborated: Mona had done none of the things she claimed for herself. Instead she had woven a web of fantasies out of the humdrum facts of her life. Far from being the assistant athletic director at her school, she was only a nutritionist in the athletic department. Her job was to help plan meals for the university's athletes. Nor was she a consultant to the Kansas City Royals; her boss at her college had merely assigned her to answer an inquiry about diet from the Royals' strength coach. She operated no firm of her own; she only had business cards printed in the hope of starting such an enterprise. She had never modeled for a New York agency; she had only participated as a teenager in a fashion show at the West Plains Country Club. She had never traveled in Europe, or much of anywhere else.

Lawrence said, "Mona spins those yarns because she thinks she should have had the kind of life they describe. She's unhappy because she knows she married the wrong man—a good man but the wrong man."

The revelations stunned Gabriel. Like her dad with his Notre Dame football, and like a whole row of ancestors unknown to her, Mona had puffed herself up with nonexistent triumphs in order to feel real. *Poor, beautiful Mona,* Gabriel thought. She might not look like a Fallon, but she had a Fallon soul—and she would haunt him from now on.

With brunch finished, Lawrence and Candace took their leave with hugs for Vonnie and Uncle Gabe. Then in the parking lot—where a woman friend of Vonnie's waited to drive him to the Springfield airport—Gabriel said his farewell to Vonnie. He embraced her and thanked her for having delivered his brother from himself.

She shook her head in denial. "But he delivered me too. I would have killed myself if Mikey hadn't come into my life. But that's another story. We saved each other, Mikey and I."

Gabriel hugged her again and then let himself into the waiting car to begin the trip home. This time Toby Myers remained silent.

CHAPTER 16

THE COMMUTER PLANE LANDED at Newburgh just after 10:00 p.m. Thea and Valerie met him with kisses, and some mockery came from Valerie about his bedraggled condition. He managed a tired grin in response. He didn't have the strength for banter. He felt relieved to be home, and he found it hard to believe that he'd been away for less than forty-eight hours. He felt as if enough had happened to fill a year.

Once in the car, Thea driving and Valerie curled up in the backseat, he began to talk, despite a weariness that seemed to have soaked into his bones. He recounted in detail the events of the funeral. He kept to himself, however, the decoding—maybe!—of the waterfall's message. There was time enough to tell Thea about that after he conducted his own test of the cascade.

All during the drive to Margaretville, through a series of Catskill thunderstorms, he heard himself babbling on. Thea and Valerie listened, saying little, sensing his need to use words to fix the past thirty hours or so in his mind. Even after they reached the house an hour and a half later, Gabriel hadn't finished. He kept talking as he drank a Coke and devoured a chicken salad sandwich. Only after midnight did he reach the end of his monologue. Valerie had fallen into a doze on the couch. Thea was fighting to stay awake. Gabriel took pity on them. "Let's go to bed."

Despite his fatigue, Gabriel lay awake. Would he again experience the voices from the motel? But only explosions of thunder invaded the room, erasing even the roar of Eternity Falls.

Despite the weather, he thought of getting up and going out by the stream to listen to the cataract. Would he hear, *Surrender to me, Gabe! Nothing really matters*? But he decided not to test the falls yet. Anything he might hear, or not hear, tonight, when weariness fogged his brain, would prove nothing. Better to try the torrent in the morning when sleep would have freshened his mind and—he hoped—fortified his spirit. Thus he stared into the blackness, Thea at his side, and waited for sleep, thankful to hear no droning Kevin, no "Danny Boy," no mockery from Toby Myers. Finally he slept.

Gabriel woke early. Crows, jays, and finches were announcing the dawn in the hemlocks beyond the bedroom window. As always, Thea was already up, making coffee in the kitchen. Valerie was no doubt still asleep. He thought, *Now is the time.*

Trying not to anticipate what might lie ahead, he pulled on jeans, a flannel shirt, and running shoes and crept downstairs. To ensure that Thea wouldn't hear him, he let himself out the front entrance rather than the kitchen door. He approached the stream. He stood on the bank where the cataract, swollen with storm water, crashed to the pool and rocks below. Shivering in a chill mist, he stared at the torrent. He let its clamor invade him. He heard something. Yes, something. But as before, it lay just beyond his ken. Then, as if bursting from a dam, the words came thundering out at him: *Surrender to me, Gabe! Nothing really matters!* He staggered back, as if an assailant had clubbed him in the chest. The words continued to roar forth: *Nothing really matters! Surrender to me Gabe!*

On and on, they went, as if they might repeat themselves through eternity. *Nothing really matters!* A knot of fear formed in Gabriel's abdomen like some malignancy. He could not deny that he heard those phrases reverberating in his ears. But did they actually emanate from the rushing water? Or did they arise from his interior, the blast of white water giving voice to the despair in his heart? *Surrender to me, Gabe!* What did it mean? Was it a call to fling himself into the eternity behind the falls? *Nothing really matters!* What did that mean? The knot of dread within him started to expand into panic. *Surrender to me, Gabe!* He imagined himself inhaling the pillar of water until death silenced it and the stream washed him away.

He pictured Thea coming upon his corpse afterward. He shuddered at the cruelty of it.

But what if the exhortation was something other than a summons to suicide? Surely you could interpret the waterfall's message in other ways. *Nothing really matters! Surrender to me Gabe!* Surely he had to consider other meanings for that message before acting on it. What if the nymph awaited him behind the wall of water to give him some gift of salvation? Nonsense maybe but what wasn't nonsense now that the falls had spoken? At this point he knew no more than the enigmatic phrases themselves and that they stirred terror in him.

Slowly, straining to overcome the gravity of the falls, he backed away from the stream bank until he stood once more outside the cloud of spray. He saw that Thea, in Columbia sweatshirt and jeans, was standing there too, had been watching him.

"What are you doing out here? You're soaked!"

Instead of answering, he seized her hand and pulled her into the mist to the falls. Hand in hand they stood on the bank. Thea looked at him in bewilderment. He listened again. *Surrender to me, Gabe!* the cascade boomed. No mistake about it. *Nothing really matters!*

Gabriel shouted above the plunging of the cataract. "Listen to it, Thea! What do you hear?"

She cocked her head. "I hear the water crashing down!" Then comprehension dawned. "You've figured out the words in the falls!" Her face glistened with the moisture in the air. "What are they?"

He shook his head and lied. "I'm not sure!" He would reveal the words to her when the time came. For now he had to keep the message to himself, to weigh further what it might portend.

Thea took him by the arm. "Come on! We need a change of clothes and a hot breakfast!" She dragged him away from the bank, out of the mist until he could no longer distinguish the words in the torrent's thunder.

Gabriel woke in darkness, his heart racing, as if he had just escaped from a nightmare, though he could remember no dream. The clock, glowing across the room, showed the time as 4:05 a.m. Thea lay deep in sleep to his left. Without waking her, he rose. He found his way to the study and opened his journal.

Time to do the necessary, to do what I have long known I must do. I have to make myself go under the cascade. I have to force myself to let that living water pound over me while I absorb its demands, so different from what I once expected. Maybe when I first conceived the idea of going into the falls, I thought of it as a poetic act, with consequences obscure and somehow romantic, a passage perhaps, as Valerie suggested. But now, having heard the words in the falling water, my going under has become a necessary act. Only by submission and courage can I confront the mysteries it harbors. It might be that God, who has rejected by his silence the proposition I put to him, will be waiting for me under that column of polar water. Will he judge me? Will he confirm what I already know, that I am only a guy who dealt in crap, a fraud who knows he deserves no mercy? Or maybe I'll find the gate to eternity under Eternity Falls and enter it hand in hand with the nymph of the falls. Or perhaps the lizard demon will be there to greet me and give me the universe. Well, why not? The world is full of mysteries, and maybe all this presents an opportunity for me to confront the biggest mystery of all: myself. Jeez, all this stuff gets more and more convoluted in my mind by the minute. Suffice it to say, I have to go under and take whatever happens. And if nothing really matters, then what have I got to lose? So why am I still so terrified of the waterfall? But I'm going. Yes. No other choice. Naturally, I haven't explained any of this to Thea. I haven't even divulged to her the words I hear in the falls. Although my heart longs to share all this with her, as I've shared everything else in our life together, I know I must keep it to myself lest she try to stop me. She already thinks I need psychiatric care. Probably she's right. But this is my test. If Thea hears about it, she might even have me committed for my own protection. So I just have to do the necessary. Alone.

Gabriel stopped writing. He looked out the window where the first light of dawn was bringing Eternity Falls to life for the new day. When would he submit himself to the ordeal? Soon. *Yeah, I'll believe that when I see it.* He recognized Toby's jeering. *You're a coward, Gabe, as well as a conceited failure. We both know it. You'll never risk your ass under that water.*

Although his previous exchanges with the resurrected Toby Myers had taken the form of interior dialogues, Gabriel now experienced such an upsurge of anger at Toby's gibe that he spoke aloud to his old companion just as he had as a boy. "Fuck you, Toby. You're just a figment."

Not a figment Gabe, a ghost, the ghost in your soul. I know all the secrets, man.

"You were supposed to be my friend, Toby, but you always hated me."

You hated yourself, pal. I was your friend. How many times did I save your ass?

"Saved? When?"

The priest in the Laff-Movie and all the other stuff? Yeah, Gabe, I took on all the dirt in your soul. Me! And what did I get out of it? You buried me, first chance you got. Yeah. Well, now I'm back, and you won't get rid of me again so easily, pal.

"What is it you want, Toby? What?"

To see that you do the necessary.

"And what is it, this necessary?"

Go under the fucking water and find out for yourself.

It came to Gabriel that if he could talk aloud to Toby as he used to, maybe he could also see him again as he once had.

"Hey, Toby! Why don't you come out and show yourself? When we were kids you weren't so shy."

But Toby had finished with him for now.

Later that day Valerie asked Gabriel if he felt all right. "I know something's going on in this house. Is it the waterfall thing?"

When Gabriel only shrugged for an answer, she said, "I get the feeling I should leave you and Ma to get on with it. Right? It's okay. I should be getting back to work anyway."

When Gabriel didn't urge her to stay, she said, "I see my duty. I'll leave tomorrow morning. Good luck, Dad."

Thea said, "I want to know what you hear in the falls." They were in bed, both naked under the blankets. She had a look of ferocity on her face. "I know you don't want to tell me, but I have to know. You owe me the truth, Gabe. Exactly what is it you're hearing?"

Reluctantly conceding the justice of her demand, he revealed the exhortation in the falls.

She repeated the words, as if turning them over in her mind. "'Surrender to me.' Sounds threatening. 'Nothing really matters.' Sounds like a cry of despair." She shuddered.

In a burst of candor he told her of his determination to go under the cataract. "I have to solve this mystery, Thea."

She clutched his hand and squeezed it as if to assure herself that he was still there by her side and still himself. "I don't want you to do this thing, Gabe. It scares me. Your heart. I'm afraid of losing you."

He held her close to him. "I have to do it."

Kneading his hand with hers, she said, "When?"

"As soon as I can find the courage. And I have to go alone. Please don't try to stop me."

She fell silent, as if weighing the revelations he had just laid on her. After a while she said, "'Surrender to me.' It doesn't have to be sinister, does it? 'Nothing really matters.' There's a lot of truth in that, isn't there? It's not necessarily threatening, is it? I want to believe that good is going to come of this." She closed her eyes as if she could no longer contemplate this thing that now would weigh on both of them until Gabriel resolved it somehow. In minutes she found refuge in sleep.

Gabriel knew she wanted to believe that good would come from all this. He wanted to believe that too. But he had no idea what awaited him, only that it filled him with dread.

CHAPTER 17

AFTER VALERIE'S BLUE TOYOTA drove up the driveway and disappeared onto the road, the house seemed eerily empty. Alone, Thea and Gabriel had little to say. Both of them understood that they now had to wait for the next act: Gabriel's immersion in the cataract.

They spent most of the day reading in the living room. Later, as the afternoon faded toward dusk in the woods beyond the windows, Gabriel thought of Michael in his coffin. How long before that box disintegrated in the Missouri earth that held it? How long before the soil absorbed Michael's mortal remains?

Thea interrupted his reverie to announce that she was going to walk down the road to visit Andrus and Ilse. She'd return in an hour, maybe two.

After she left, Gabriel went out to the waterfall. By now the shadows had deepened even more under the hemlocks and mountain maples. But the heat of the day persisted. A cloud of moisture hovered about the falling water.

The moment had come.

He approached the torrent within its mist. Halting on the bank, he listened to it. The words spilled out. *Surrender to me, Gabe. Nothing really matters.* Taut with determination, Gabriel stripped naked. He felt icy droplets pelting his skin. A breeze passed through the hollow. He thought, *This is the time.*

He found himself wondering where Toby Myers was now.

I'm here, where I belong. I'm always here, watching you, pal. This is the moment.

Gabriel stared at the liquid pillar before him. What might lie hidden behind that curtain of white?

Go on, coward. Push on. Listen to your old buddy. Do the necessary.

Again Gabriel challenged Toby to show himself. "Okay, Toby, if you're my pal, I dare you to come out now. Like the old days, let me see you, Toby. Help me."

I'm trying to help you, pal, like I always did. So quit your stalling, Gabe. Listen to your old buddy. You wasted your life, and now you got to have the guts to do the necessary.

"Then you ought to have the guts to come out, Toby. Let me see if you still wear those Coke-bottle glasses. Are you still a crippled shrimp, you mean little bastard?"

I'm your friend, Gabe, trying to help you.

Out of the corner of his eye, Gabriel spied a movement in the brush on the other side of the stream. Had Toby Myers accepted his dare to make himself visible? Gabriel definitely detected someone there behind the bushes. Moving eyes, dark curls, a diminutive form. A boy hiding there?

Gabriel called out. "I see you, Toby! Come out, you creep!" But Toby ran off. Had it really been him? But it could have been no one else.

Whatever the case, the incident had shattered Gabriel's resolve to test the cataract that day. He gathered his clothes and went back to the house. Toby, keeping himself invisible, called after him: *Gutless!*

That night, at dinner, Thea said, "Well?"

Gabriel knew what she wanted to know. He said, "I'll have to try another time."

In bed with Thea, Gabriel dreamed of the worlds that whirled on the other side of Eternity Falls. Once again the nymph invited him to pass through the gates and the demon lizard offered him the universe behind the shield of falling water—if he would only do the necessary. This time, however,

Gabriel heard no urgency, no fear, no Toby calling from the void. He woke feeling refreshed.

Despite its ambiguity, the dream felt reassuring, as if to say that whatever happened under the waterfall, it would all work out for the best. He reflected on how much his life had become an effort to make sense of the fantastic.

With the dawn seeping into the bedroom, Thea and Gabriel made love, long, sweet, and wet. Passionate in his embrace, Thea whispered, "Don't let the waterfall take you."

Every day Gabriel went out and stood by the stream, as if waiting for another moment of urgency to compel him into the water again. None came. Every day as he stood waiting, he summoned Toby to come forth, but Toby not only failed to show himself, he had gone silent. Gabriel would call into the woods: "Hey, Toby! Who's the gutless one here?" Once in a while he would catch a glimpse of a furtive motion in the shadows beneath the trees—Toby, of course, skulking about and watching. But Toby refused to respond to Gabriel's taunting.

Every day Gabriel wrote in his journal, recording the passing of time, noting Toby's withdrawal, his own continuing dread of the waterfall. Before he realized it, July had slipped into August. The days, golden now, grew shorter, the nights chillier. He wrote in his journal:

I'm still gutless. Has Toby deserted me at the climax?

A few periods of light rain swelled the falls perceptibly. Gabriel knew that if a week of really heavy weather set in, the cataract would grow so violent it would become impossible to stand beneath it. Was he secretly hoping for that to happen? An excuse to evade the necessary?

On a Sunday afternoon Richard called to say that the problem between Benji and the neighbor boy had dissolved; a court had placed the boy in a home for disturbed children.

Gabriel said, "Let's hope it works out for the poor kid."

Richard said, "Did you ever hear from God?"

"No."

"Maybe you did and don't realize it."

His words sent a chill through Gabriel. Could it be God calling for him after all? To inform him that nothing really matters? Was that what he was afraid of? Revelation? He wrote in his journal:

Approaching the end of August. It's actually cold at night now. Winter is already breathing over these hills. If I don't act soon I'll always be where I am now, hanging between despair and nowhere. Poor Thea, having to put up with me. Toby's silence continues. Do it! We all die, Stupid.

Valerie called with news that she had put her potential love affair on hold. "We agreed to think things over. Have you gone under the waterfall, Dad?"

"Not yet."

"Do it, Dad. I want you to write again. Do it."

Everybody wanted him to do the necessary.

One night as he awaited sleep at Thea's side, Gabriel solved the mystery that had baffled him for weeks: the identity of the real Toby Myers. With a precision that eradicated all doubt, Gabriel's memory reconstructed how Toby—Tobias, to give his Christian name—had entered his life and mind.

It had started when young Gabe, still a newcomer to the Keller household, was perusing the photographs that Mrs. Keller kept displayed on a wall of her parlor and noticed a certain, vaguely familiar face among them. Closer scrutiny told young Gabe that the face belonged to the boy who had waved a greeting from the upstairs window on the day that he and Michael had arrived at the Keller home. Only young Gabe had seen the face in the window, and then for only a second or two, but he recognized it with certainty in the black-and-white photograph on the wall.

Fascinated, he spent several minutes studying the photo—on which someone had written "Tobias Myers" in white ink. The picture showed Tobias Myers, who looked about nine or ten, posed in bright sunshine on a lawn somewhere. Tobias Myers was squinting through thick glasses and scowling as if angry at having his picture taken. He was wearing high-top sneakers, corduroy knickers, and a light-colored short-sleeve shirt. His dark hair looked like a mass of curls, and he was skinny like young Gabe himself. The thing that young Gabe noticed most about Tobias Myers, however, was his withered right arm. It hung from his shoulder as if someone had stuck a monkey's arm onto his boy body. In addition, the hand at the end of the monkey arm curled up like a fist. Young Gabe understood: Tobias Myers was a victim of the dreaded polio.

As he stared at the photo, young Gabe found himself wondering who this Tobias Myers might be. Why did he rate a photograph on Mrs. Keller's parlor wall? What had he done? Where was he now? Why and how had he waved from the window that day of young Gabe's advent among the Kellers?

In his perplexity young Gabe had turned to his fourteen-year-old hero Jake Keller for information about Tobias Myers. As he had supposed, Jake knew most of the answers: Toby—as Jake called the crippled boy—had boarded with the Kellers the previous summer. "Sad sort of fella, that Toby. Nasty too sometimes. He'd sneak up and hit you with that gimpy arm, try to get you mad so's you'd finally lose patience and smack him back. Then he'd go bawling off to tell on you for hittin' a cripple." Jake shook his head as if recalling such incidents. "And if you'd try to be nice to Toby, he'd turn even meaner and sneakier. Yeah, it was hard to be nice to Toby, but my ma took a shine to him, even against me." Again Jake shook his head, clearly still mystified at his mother's liking for the cripple.

Young Gabe asked what Toby Myers had done to deserve a picture in the parlor.

Jake grinned. "Jumped into that old quarry full of water up there on the mountain, just like he wasn't supposed to, and he drowned. I'm the one found him up there, floating all by himself in that slime water, all his clothes still on him. State troopers said it wasn't my ma's fault. One of 'em even said it looked like the boy drowned himself. On purpose. My ma put his picture up there on the wall, Tobias Myers. Like a memorial."

Jake flashed another grin and asked why young Gabe wanted to know about Toby Myers. For a second young Gabe had considered telling how he had seen Toby's face in the window, but he thought better of it and just shrugged his shoulders.

Still grinning, Jake, who had a taste for the macabre, offered the information that, when alive, Toby had slept in the same room and bed where Gabe was sleeping now. "Maybe he's haunting you." Young Gabe had joined Jake in laughing at such an absurdity.

In bed that night, however, he had lain awake thinking of Toby Myers. What if his ghost was present in the room that had been his? What if Toby Myers felt lonely, lost, abandoned, just as young Gabe himself so often did? What if Toby Myers regretted the impulse that had caused him to jump into the quarry? What if, like Gabe, he needed someone to understand his hurt?

Moved by an upsurge of sympathy, young Gabe had whispered the name. "Toby Myers."

An answer came at once. *I'm here.*

And so it had begun.

Now, as a man four decades later, Gabriel whispered again into the darkness of another bedroom. "Toby, don't hide anymore. Come out. I'm sorry I put all this weight on you. I know you're out there in the woods. I catch glimpses of you when I go to the falls. You don't have to hide from me, not from me."

As he had so many years before, Toby replied at once. *I'm here, pal.*

CHAPTER 18

O N A DRIZZLY SATURDAY afternoon Gabriel went again to the waterfall. Thea was shopping in Margaretville. He stood on the bank and listened to the thunder of the water, swollen from a morning of rain. Suddenly the sun emerged. It turned the white of the cataract to a softer ivory. The drizzle abated.

Without willing it, Gabriel slipped into the stream—already glacial with the onrushing season of cold. Clothed in running shoes, jeans, and a gray sweatshirt, he strained to maintain his balance in the current. He thought, *I'm here, I'm in.*

Heart beating wildly, he advanced a few steps in the thigh-high flow toward the torrent that roared out of the ravine above him. He paused, feeling the icy spray on his face and hands. He had never come this close to the cascade before. His heart shuddered at the sight and sound of it. From his vantage point in the stream the liquid pillar seemed to wash from the sky. He craned his neck to gaze up to the top of it. Masses of dark water far above him gathered, writhed over a ledge of granite and then plunged down to explode on the rocks below—rocks that now lay only a few yards away from where he stood in the current.

Viewed from so close, the falling water seemed otherworldly. Despite the dread knotting his chest, Gabriel resumed his approach to it. With each step the cataract became higher, more powerful, until it seemed to clamor simultaneously from the forest, the sky, and the under-earth itself. But where was the nymph of the falls, the gate behind the veil of water, the demon lizard? Above all, where were the words in the water? Why had the cataract muted its message at this climactic moment? Were the words a delusion after all?

Gabriel halted again in the flow. His calves and toes were starting to lose feeling in the freezing rush, now up to his waist. The bursting water made the streambed tremble beneath his feet. He inhaled deeply in an attempt to calm his heart. He told himself, *This is the time.* He wanted Toby. He needed Toby. There could be no finish without Toby. He called out for him. "Toby, where are you? Help me now!" But the blast of the falls overwhelmed his plea. Raw spray filled the air. To preserve some of his body heat, he clasped his arms across his chest. All right, he told himself, now that he had embarked. He had no choice but to submit himself to the prodigy before him. Now was the time. To grasp the mystery, he had to give himself to it—at once—and he had to accept whatever it dealt him.

Again stepping toward the wall of water, he thought, *This is the necessary. Endure it.* Quickly, lest his courage fail, he thrust his head and shoulders under the torrent. The force of it flung him to his knees. The flood beat upon him as he knelt beneath it. It drenched him through his clothing. It froze his ears and scalp. After a few seconds, unable to rise, he managed to crawl backward out of the turbulence. He shook with a cold that penetrated his core like a thousand needles. He struggled to his feet. See it through now, see it through. Embrace it all. Do the necessary. But where are you, Toby?

Following what he perceived as the next step in a process, Gabriel stripped off his soaked clothes. He flung them into the current. They whirled away downstream. Naked and trembling uncontrollably now, he forced himself to reenter the thundering pillar. He fought to keep his body upright beneath the weight that hurled itself down on him. A fist of ice squeezed his heart. The world, and time, contracted to this place and moment—the rushing power of it, the deafening roar of it, the interstellar cold of it, the ceaselessness of it, the eternal wet of it. All crashed about in his head: ceaseless thunder, age of ages, the cleansing power, the shock that restoreth.

As Gabriel strove to hold himself erect under the cascade, it came to him that the water striking against his head was in truth passing into his skull and through his body, as if he were a tube open at both ends. Now, at last, he heard Toby: *Washed in the eternal.*

With his core nearing insensibility, and unable any longer to bear up under the burden of the water, Gabriel dropped to his knees again. As the cataract tore through his body, he readied himself to capitulate to the force that held him in its grip, prepared to release himself to it. At this moment he heard—whole and clear—the words in the falling water: *Surrender to me, Gabe. Nothing really matters. Nothing really matters. Nothing really matters.* He could no longer breathe. Fluid numbed his nose and mouth. He thought, *I'm drowning.*

Gabriel descried a figure on the stream bank. Toby, visible at last, Toby in his knickers and long-sleeved shirt, Toby present at the climax. Over the clamor of water Gabriel heard Toby call to him. *Surrender Gabe. Nothing really matters. You wasted your life, now do the necessary.*

But Thea.

Do the necessary, pal. Surrender. Now.

Gabriel forced his expiring body to its feet. He tottered under his icy burden. He had a choice to make: to use the last strength of his body, the body that was only going to be his for the next few seconds, to extract himself from the waterfall's grip—or to let the flood coursing through him drain away his life. Nothing really matters. Breathless, he thought, *But it does matter, does matter.*

Compared to the life he'd lived, his failure was a trivial matter. Gabriel had not wasted his life. It did matter, his life. Even his failure mattered because it was part of his life. How could he have thought otherwise? Now he had to hurl himself out of Eternity Falls—into the world of sun where life dwelt, where Thea dwelt.

Calling up a last shred of strength, he strained to move his body from under its burden. Toby appeared, under the cascade, at his side, soaked and grinning. His crippled arm encircled Gabriel's neck. Toby said, *Too late, pal. You had your chance.*

Gabriel struggled but found he was hollow now, washed clean of blood and brain—an empty skin in Toby's grip. Toby said, *This is the necessary, pal. From now on we'll be together. Together.*

The darkness seeped in. The waterfall fell silent. Gabriel entered a bowl of space where the demon lizard hung in the blackness—at the end of time.

EPILOGUE

THEA WENT OUT TO take a last look at Eternity Falls where so much she'd thought endless had come to an end, including the happiness (so rare!) that she had shared with the dreamy young man who had become the wounded older man she loved. *All that is gone now,* she thought. But the thought held no bitterness—for she had grieved the bitterness out of her heart.

As she gazed at the waterfall, Thea reflected that it seemed no more lethal now than it had before it killed Gabriel—or rather before Gabriel had used it to kill himself. Although the autumn rains had increased its volume twofold, the falls seemed to Thea a benign presence in the gloom of the surrounding forest. She heard no baleful words in its music. But of course she never had. Only Gabriel had detected the summons he answered.

Once again Thea pondered the lesson she had drawn from Gabriel's fate: every interior life takes place in an exotic landscape; every soul's history is a fantasy tale. Even she, who had loved him more than life, could not have entered Gabriel's interior, could not have averted the climax he had chosen for his tale. She took an acidic comfort in that reality.

A breath of the approaching winter gusted through the hemlocks, causing her to pull her jacket tighter. Soon a sheath of ice would muffle the falls, but she wouldn't be here to appreciate the silence; she would be living in Chicago with her son and his family. Grandma Fallon would be swamped in the love of her children and grandchildren. In fact, Richard would back the Jeep out of the garage any minute now, and they would then drive off to catch the plane for Chicago. She would never behold Eternity Falls, or these woods, or this strange house again—unless in dreams.

And so in these last minutes before departure, she had come out to the stream to impress on her memory not only a final image of the cataract but also to reflect once more on what had happened here, beneath Eternity Falls. Thus, as she had so often over the past weeks, Thea pictured the event as the authorities had reconstructed it:

A man, Thea's man, Gabriel Fallon, naked and in severe hypothermia, is on his knees under the pounding torrent, which he has entered for reasons that will remain forever unknown to later investigators who will eventually ascribe his act to mental derangement. Gasping with exhaustion, the man struggles to escape the burden of water, but his fibrillating heart proves unequal to the task. Meanwhile, hidden behind some bushes on the far bank of the stream, a boy of eleven watches, uncomprehending, as the naked man, shouting and shaking, writhes in agony beneath the cascade. The boy is not sure what to do. The man is clearly in need of help. But the boy, who has been trespassing and fishing in the stream out of season, is afraid of harsh punishment if he reveals himself by plunging into the stream to help the naked man. So, heart hammering, the boy watches—as he has on other days when the man has spotted him, shouted at him, and sent him running. But this time the man is in trouble.

The boy steps out from behind the bushes. The man shouts at him. The words mean nothing to the boy. But this time he does not run away. The man is drowning. The boy knows he must try to save him.

The boy jumps into the freezing current. Suddenly the man collapses under the waterfall. The boy pushes on toward the big pale body, now bobbing beneath the torrent like a deer carcass. His plan is to pull the man from under the falls, float him to the bank, and then run for help—for he knows that the man's lady is not in the big house.

But when the boy tries to take hold of the man's shoulders, the man seizes the boy by the neck. His weight crushes the boy, presses him under. The boy kicks, thrashes his arms. But he can't get loose. He is drowning.

Then the man's grip loosens. The boy breathes again. The man rolls onto his back, his eyes still open. The boy, gasping, lurches out of the stream and staggers away in search of help.

The naked man, still on his back, washes out of the falls. He drifts downstream until he comes to rest against a boulder, where the local rescue squad later finds him dead.

After their investigation the authorities will conclude that the man died because his heart gave out. That alone saved the boy from drowning in his struggle with the man. Instead of punishment, the boy—who suffered a broken right arm in his rescue attempt—will receive much praise for his bravery. The dead man's actions will remain a mystery.

So Gabriel's story had ended in a climax that made sense—if it made any sense at all—to him alone. For Thea now the task was to hold tight to the life she had shared with him.

All at once, for no reason she could discern, there came into her mind a memory of her first date with Gabriel. They had gone to Coney Island on the subway. She had worn a miniskirt to show off her legs. Gabriel had won prize after prize at the arcade games. How fine it had been that night, and so many nights afterward. How fine!

She heard the Jeep's horn, Richard signaling that it was time to go.

It was over then, certainly and forever, but it lived on in her—so much life. She turned away from Eternity Falls to join Richard in the car. She thought how lucky she had been, how rare to have been so happy for so long. And how grateful she would always be for that.